G000069898

To Tony and Annie,

A Country of
Vanished Dreams

with fond regards,

[illegible]

PHILIP BREBNER

A Country of Vanished Dreams

PICADOR
Published by Pan Books

First published in 1992 by Pan Books Ltd,
Cavaye Place, London SW10 9PG
135798642

ISBN 0 330 32178 1

Phototypeset by Intype, London
Printed in Great Britain by
Billing & Sons Ltd, Worcester

Grateful acknowledgement is made to Penguin Books for permission to quote from the following

Farid ud-Din Attar. *The Conference of the Birds.*
Trans. Afkham Darbandi and Dick Davis. 1984.

The Song of Roland. Trans. Glyn Burgess. 1990.

Frantz Fanon. *The Wretched of the Earth.*
Trans. Constance Farringdon. 1967.

The Koran. Trans. N. J. Dawood.

Poems in Chapter 2 translated from:
A. Memmi, *La Poésie algérienne de 1830 à nos jours: Approches socio-historique.* Paris, Mouton. 1963.

Pierre Louys. *Bilitis.*

AUTHOR'S NOTE

Most of this novel is based on my own research and personal knowledge of Algeria. However, I am indebted to: Bourdieu, P., *Equisse d'une théorie de la pratique*, Librairie Droz, 1972: Horne, A., *A Savage War of Peace, Algeria 1954–1962*, Macmillan, 1977: *Lettres du Maréchal de Saint-Arnaud*, 1855, Vol. 1 & 2.: Berard, Jh-P, *Les deux villes de Ténès et Bou-Maza*, 1864: Desparmet, J., 'L'Oeuvre de la France en Algérie jugée par les indigènes, *Bulletin de la Société de géographie d'Alger et de l'Afrique du Nord*', Vol 15, No. 2 & 4, 1910: Le RPA Giacobetti des Pères Blancs, *Recueil d'énigmes arabes populaires*, Aldolphe Jourdan, Algiers, 1916; and various numbers of *Les Temps modernes*.

I include also Sir Richard Burton's translation of *The Book of the Thousand and One Nights*.

To my parents, Lily and George,
e também a Virgínia e Domingos.

January 1987

If the crowded pavement allowed you to pause to consider the façade of the building, it would appear as many others appear: a ghost of the French era in Algiers. But cross the street to try to enter, and a tall, barrel-chested man wearing a tin mask, hiding a lost face, will stand suddenly from the shadows of the vestibule in his brown burnous like a hooded hawk, and in stridulant Arabic demand from you a special pass. Only after his approval will the elegant, double iron doors be permitted to open, barely illuminating the red-and-jet terrazzo veiled by the layered gloom of the unlit foyer beyond. Then there, after a few doubtful steps, you can snatch at the gleam of a polished timber rail, and quickly ascend the spacious staircase which curves up to the offices lined along the first floor.

'Lieutenant Haddad, Colonel Bedjami will speak to you now.'

The noise of the traffic from outside brushed and stippled colour into the greyness of the room. Hung upon the far wall was a portrait of president Chadli Bendjedid, with grandfatherly white hair and a sharp blue three-piece suit. The colonel sat beneath this at a metal desk. Haddad stood to attention, and saluted.

'At ease, Lieutenant. I would ask you to sit down, but, as you see, there are no chairs. A conference, I believe.'

'Sir! My father asked me to convey his regards.'

Colonel Bedjami nodded. He began to revolve a gold propelling pencil between surprisingly delicate fingers. Beside him a Havana cigar smouldered, untouched, in a saucer.

'The November riots in Constantine: four died; one hundred and eighty-six were arrested. The charges varied from disturbance of the peace, to damage to property; the sentences ranged from two to eight years. I wonder if the students find life in their cells any better than the tuition and living conditions they protested about? What do you think, Lieutenant?'

'Enemies of the state, sir.'

'No, Lieutenant. Pawns.'

'Yes, sir. Pawns, sir.'

His superior continued twisting the propelling pencil. 'Later the security services hunted out and detained three academics and a lawyer thought to have been behind the riots. These I rank as the real enemies of the state. However, we suspect a fifth evaded us.' He opened a file, and spoke in a new voice. 'Muhammad Madani. Born 1952 in Tougourt. At Constantine University studied history . . .'

A wave of dates and facts drilled at school, and inculcated by the media, surged over Lieutenant Haddad. The demise of Turkish rule and the capture of Algiers by the French in 1830; the Setif bloodbath in 1945; the war of Independence in 1954, Independence in 1962, the coup by Houari Boumédienne in 1965. History had been a constant struggle in which there were some winners, some losers, and some traitors. Haddad had disliked history at school, and this antipathy he now constructively targeted onto Muhammad Madani.

'He's turned up at El Oued. Innocent though he might be, personally I'd trump up a charge to arrest him now. However, the word is that President Chadli is going to pardon all those connected with the riots later this year as part of the twenty-fifth year of Independence celebrations.'

Unannounced, a shaft of sun burst into the office, lighting clouds of hanging dust.

'Sir! You require me to make a file on him?'

'It's a little more complicated than that. During the week he works in the packaging room at a date factory in Le Souf, a few kilometres away. He then plays the role of Rahwun the story-teller at the Friday market. It seems he pulls quite a crowd.'

'Unlawful assembly, sir!'

'Story-tellers have wandered Algeria as long as anyone can remember. Of course, it's difficult to prove subversiveness from a tangle of tales, songs, riddles, and whatever else. What worries us is that he might start peddling it around other towns, such as Ouargla, or Laghouat. It could spell the end of the Front de Libération Nationale as the sole political party of the state. Extremists are lurking everywhere, and the young are hungry for a cult hero. Their ingratitude to their elders and the FLN galls me. Sad is the day when the children of our revolution become our enemies. Lieutenant, you volunteered for this assignment, I believe?'

'Yes, sir. A woman, sir.'

'Your reasons are your own. But two to three months in El Oued will not be easy. You are required to attend these weekly performances; also, see what else you can add to his file. Any action we may take against Madani will be decided on your final report and recommendation.'

'Sir!'

The colonel pushed a manila envelope across the desk. 'Air tickets. Hotel reservations. Identity. And our dossier to date.'

Outside, a moped stuttered by. A nod from the colonel indicated that the interview was over. Lieutenant Haddad saluted, tucked the envelope under his arm, turned and left.

Clouds shifted and vied with the sun for the winter day. The lieutenant plunged into the push of the thoroughfare; eventually his slow advance brought him to the Café Brazzaville. Inside he chose a seat adjacent to the window.

'Shoeshine?'

Haddad declined. The gaunt-faced young man took his wooden box and services elsewhere. A waiter appeared from behind, emptied the ashtray on to the floor, and ran a stained cloth over the top of the table.

'One coffee.'

The manila envelope had not been sealed. Before withdrawing the contents, the lieutenant tapped out a cigarette from a packet of Gauloises, and lit it. The coffee arrived in a tiny chipped cup. He stirred in sugar from a sachet printed with the logo of the state food-processing giant, SN-SEMPAC.

The dossier on Muhammad Madani was brief. He had been exempted from military service (reason unspecified). He had a brother working in Paris, and he had travelled overseas six times. He had been an active member of various student groups at university. An application for a grant to pursue a doctorate at the University of Aix-Marseille had been refused. He was married with two children, both girls.

A passport-size black-and-white photograph revealed a

balding man with a triangular face, a serious mouth, and strong eyebrows above dark, incisive eyes.

An identity card had been made out for Lieutenant Haddad with the alias of Sliman Djerri. A telex in this name confirmed a reservation for an indefinite stay at the Hôtel El Souf in El Oued. The red and white *Air Algérie* ticket indicated that Sliman Djerri was due to fly to El Oued very early the next morning.

'A postcard, sir, or a pen?'

Irritated, Haddad waved away the kid and his cardboard tray of odds and ends.

Most people turning at the heights of the Place Addis Ababa, on to Avenue Boudjemaa Souidani, would try to glimpse the view of Algiers as it drops with the beauty and chaos of an avalanche to the curve of the bay and the blueness of the Mediterranean Sea. Lieutenant Haddad, however, glanced right to the whitewashed edifice of the British Council, for fifteen months ago he had enrolled in English classes there, and had met Anissa, a student at the Institute of Law. She had pretty features; she had a good figure; but what had attracted Haddad to her most of all was her candour. It thrilled him when she referred to the party leaders as 'the dinosaurs' or was scathing about his sports car, Swiss watch and polo shirts by Lacoste. Too soon she had left to spend the summer vacation with her family in the Kabylie, three months in which they had yearned for each other in a way they had interpreted as love, yet they had voiced their feelings only once, not in Arabic, not in French, but in English:

'Haddad, I love you.'

'I am loving you also.'

And they had laughed together at the strangeness of it.

The lieutenant turned his red coupé off the road, and hammered his horn twice at a wide, solid gate. It was swung open by an old man in a skull cap.

Palm trees, swaying gently in the wind, lined the approach to the villa. He stopped the car, trotted up the steps edged by spilling ferns and gloss-leafed rubber trees, and strode into the house, calling his sister.

'Layla!'

He heard the clip-clopping of high heels hurry along the tiled floor of a corridor towards him. His mood was little tempered when he saw her.

'What's that on your face?'

'A little mascara and lipstick. That's all.'

'So this is what you get up to when our parents go to visit our brother in America! Aren't you ashamed? Other girls your age have to stay at home, yet this is how you abuse the privilege of being allowed to study. I'll be seeing you hang around the cafés along the Didouche Mourad smoking next! Take that muck off at once, then pack your things.'

'What do you mean, "pack your things"?'

'Until our father comes back, you're off to stay at our uncle's in El Biar. He's collecting you this evening after Il-Maghrib prayer. I've been ordered away.'

'Eloping with your sweetheart?'

'Dream away.'

The cook had appeared at the kitchen door, and looked bewildered. Haddad shouted, 'And you, get me an omelette. And a banana!' and with that he stalked into the study.

On the oak desk was a framed photograph of his father, taken with the late President Boumédienne. From a left-hand drawer Haddad took a sheet of writing paper.

Dear Anissa,

Sighing, he lit a cigarette, leant back in the leather chair, and gazed out of the arched windows across the terrace to the pool, and the lawn beyond. There was a rap on the door.

'What is it?'

'Your omelette—'

'Feed it to the cats!'

This hour before the twilight had brought a soft, violet sky. Reaching across from the crystal ashtray, Haddad switched on the desk lamp, less for necessity than for the solace of its sallow light.

> This is a very difficult letter for me to send to you. I am going away for some weeks, and when I return I am to be married before Ramadan. My mother has been plotting my marriage since I was eighteen. I managed to out-manoeuvre her for seven years until a few months ago when she told me that she had chosen a girl from a well-connected family who would make a very suitable wife. I refused to even consider the match, but all sorts of pressure was put on me until finally I had to agree. I know this will be a shock, and I am sorry. I know we made plans, and even talked about children. But at the end of the day we have to face up to reality.

He sucked the top of his biro, pondering a suitable valedictory message. Finally he wrote:–

I am loving you also.

Haddad

Sliman Djerri walked through into the lobby of the Hôtel El Souf and left his key at reception. He was unshaven, wound with a turban and wrapped in a white burnous, bought during his reconnaissance of El Oued the previous day. The volumes of woollen cloth not only made him less conspicuous amongst the local population, but hid the compact Sony recorder slung from his waist.

The sky was fresh and clear. Haddad turned past the post-office into the Avenue Talib Larbi, bordered by the low, domed buildings of adobe which chequered the Saharan town. To his left, a little distance from a rank of taxis, the street opened into a vast market place. Hillocks of oranges, baskets of green vegetables, noisy herds of sheep and goats, were all united by clusters of people in a frenzy of haggling. Aimlessly, Haddad meandered about. He found El Oued tedious and provincial and he missed his car. At that moment a man near by drew a circle in the sand with the point of a stick; standing back, he took off his sandals, and placed one to his left and one to his right, and then squatted between them. Haddad kept his distance as he watched, but as soon as the man threw the cowl of his burnous from his head, he recognized him as Muhammad Madani. Already four or five others had congregated before him. Haddad strolled across. Another two joined the group. Madani closed his eyes and began a low, melodic chant, and around him the crowd continued to gather.

Then he spoke.

Unnoticed, Lieutenant Haddad switched on his tape-recorder.

The First

So I look tired? Well, I've had a bleak night of sleeplessness, and far worse, it roused my wife. O truly, the most serious problems are the small ones!

Yes, yes, inshallah!, I'll still spin thee some new and pretty yarn. But therein lies my predicament: how to begin, or with what? With dispossession? With displacement? Or even: with honour? Maybe with the fight for freedom, perhaps with the twisting of dreams?

Or . . . with who? France?

Or with whom? Bashir and Jamila? Nadia or her son Azallah? With the good servant Siddiq, or with Yamina? With the Field Marshal, Saint-Arnaud, and the infamies of his illustrious career? With Si Abd Allah, or . . .

No, there is no Sindbad the Seaman, nor a Scheherazade.

Wa-llahi! With the marabout Si Abd Allah. I shall open with him. Sahha! Gather, a little closer; more of you can sit if you wish.

'. . . mind those sheep droppings . . .'

'Come on, be quiet the lot of you! Let Rahwun begin.'

Hu-hem: I'll just clear my throat. H-hm!

I give you a story, and I have not come to see you. Some tell of the people of a country . . . but to me they are crutches, for it is neither people, nor a country: it is only Allah that can Be. If I lie, Allah pardon me, whereas if it is the devil, let Allah damn him. There was . . . there was not. There is basil and there are lilies in the lap of the Prophet, may Allah bless him and grant him peace. O you who listen to this tale, my narrative is beautiful and fabulous and tragic, and travels back and forth through time. And benedictions on the Prophet, the Friend! In the name of Allah, the Compassionate, the Merciful!

It is still there. The simple domed cube, the shrine of the marabout, Si Abd Allah.

Yes, it is still there, its whiteness patched by neglect, as sad and noble and solitary as the Algerian landscape which overwhelms it.

O so you recall the proverb: how many a saint's tomb is the object of pilgrimages whilst its occupant rots in hell?

Not Si Abd Allah. For he is certainly among the righteous who recline in the exquisiteness of the gardens of Paradise.

He was born in the month of Rabi ith-thani, a September (or, if you prefer, Vendémiaire, as it was that exact same month that the French Republic was declared with hope in its heart and nothing but the motto Liberté, Egalité, et Fraternité in its mouth). It was the year 1207 AH, 1792 AD (or Year One of the short-lived Republican Calendar).

But here, so soon, I dice with being called to order as a braggart of erudition, so swiftly I continue on and say: Algeria was at that time a regency of the Ottoman Empire, and Si Abd Allah grew up in a village in the beylic of Qusantina.

It was Sheikh al-Mahmoud who led him to a state of holiness, in Si Abd Allah's eighteenth year, in the season when the carob trees blossom petalless flowers like strings of beads of blood. He was guided, climbing, fumbling, sometimes stumbling, to the very mightiest Kabylie mountain range, Lalla Khedidja, to a crevice chosen for its dimensions which were such that a man could neither stand nor lie. He wriggled in and was entombed by a wall of stones, with a spiracle for receipt of air and food and Si Abd Allah came to know that space, his finger tips travelled each curve, every smoothness, some raggedness, and slid up into its single deep cleft.

And lo! During forty days his food was gradually reduced, to but one fig, which he would prise apart with his thumbs to lick the flowered flesh within, to but a little water, sipped, given each day in the sunset's blush.

This was a measure of his existence, as were the moments when the airy glory of a sunbeam shattered the shadows, then vanished, leaving him swathed in that obscurity which hazes Life from the precipice-edge of Death.

Although contorted by cramp, and stifled by the stench of sweat and defecation, he was cleansed within by fasting, and comforted by his rote of verses from the Holy Qur'an . . . *I seek refuge in the Lord of men, the King of men, the God of men, from the mischief of the slinking prompter who whispers in the heart of men, from jinn and men.* Until finally Abd Allah lost his relation with material life, and drifted into a pageant of dreams and visions.

Sheikh al-Mahmoud waited to hear tell of some second sight which would most perfectly coincide with the most secret of his own. He heard of hag-faced sorceresses who tied tangled knots in a cord and spat on them with a spoken curse. He listened to dreams of splendent angels, of houri virgins, and of half-human and half-animal jinn. He was foretold of a sanguinary battle, a city with onion-shaped cupolas set aflame, and untold dead in the splintered crystal and maggot-white ravages of winter.

Patiently, serenely, Sheikh al-Mahmoud waited.

And then he heard tell of the black smudge of a locust cloud swooping from the north. He heard of a vision of birds in flight through countless skies stippling the heavens. He heard of a dream of glistening and red-gilled fishes, journeying beneath the spume-flecked surface of the seas.

This was kindling: it needed yet flint to strike steel.

The day fell. Crickets chirruped and the fireflies danced gold pentagrams against night.

At last, with the pallor of the dawn, came the whispered image of a wind spiralled into a cone, spun between continents, and which grasped tight the hearts of many.

Flint struck steel. Sparks blazed as brilliant as a peacock's tail into a mystical affinity between master and novice. The initiation was over; the crevice was opened up. Sheikh al-Mahmoud gave Si Abd Allah a stout stick, banded in brass and inscribed with verses of the Qur'an, a sign of his investiture, and sent him forth into the world to make converts . . .

'But . . . ya Rahwun: the vision, the dream, the whispered image, what do they mean?'

Perhaps a few coins before me might reveal that which you wish to know . . . Shukran, shukran: such generosity, al-hamdu li–llah!

'And so, what do they mean?'

I trust that you will be content with the proverb: live and you will see—

– for it is six years on that my story continues. The time when Lord Exmouth led a force of the British Navy, bolstered by a Dutch squadron, to put paid to those impertinent pups and upstarts, the Algiers pirates, the fleet's broadside of cannonfire blasting the city into heaps of rubbish from the waves, sweet-talking a refund of monies extorted from the Italian states, and gaining the liberty of two thousand Christian slaves. And whilst the Dey of Algiers, Omar, was merrily strangled for this capitulation, the Black Death, inactive for fourteen years, once again resurged with its suppurating buboes in the north-east of Algeria.

Wah! It was that summer, that summer that a baby boy was born, far south by the Niger, and with his first scream an ostrich ran alarmed, with a kick of dust, and its wings outspread, tracing a great circle whilst the child was named Siddiq, meaning, I remind you, someone as trustworthy as he is faithful.

It was a portent of his future.

But here I fly on, passing over eleven Ramadans, to a dispute arising in connection with some wheat that two Jews of Algiers, Bacri and Busnach, had supplied to the Directory. Impassioned, Hassan, the ruling Dey, graced the French consul-general Deval with the pretty compliment *wicked, faithless, idol-worshipping rascal*, and the flick of his flywhisk . . .

Thwack!

Eleven Ramadans, and the longest rainbow, childhood, dissolves.

For back below the Tropic of Cancer, in head-dresses and veils of wound white cloth, in robes blued by indigo dye, Tuareg slave-traders tremored the stillness, champed the silence as they galloped, standing in their stirrups, on sweat-glossed stallions, towards the salt lake glittering by Taoudenni. A report from a rifle deterred escape, and collapsed into fragments the eggshell existences of the sprinkling of men who hacked salt from shallow scars in the crust. Siddiq, the youngest of these salt-collectors, stopped baling water and stood, his spindly black-skinned body shivering in the sun. As the Tuaregs ringed around the trenches, Siddiq turned as his shoulders were hugged by his father.

Said he, Siddiq: 'Ya baba, I am filled with fear.'

Said he, his father: 'Be calm and keep Allah next to your heart. And remember that Islam promises recompense for the slave on the Day of Judgement and requires kindness from a master, al-hamdu li-llah.'

Wrists bound by leather, rubbing raw his skin and squeezing violent tears, Siddiq was taken southwards on foot, till from the dunes, mimosas, and acacia trees bulged the jumbled dilapidation of hand-sculpted hand-smoothed coppery mud buildings which gnarled the streets and alleys of Timbuctoo. There, with other children, with women and with men, Siddiq was sold, his and each life valued at – no bagatelle – the weight of sixteen quintels of dates. A kindly smile from his father was the memory of a man he was never to see again.

Let me pause here—

'—for more money?'

What cynicism when all I wish is to pose a riddle! I give you to guess: our slave is green, and bears children which are born white and turn black. Puzzled? You want the answer? Not yet: but if you're impatient, digesting it a little will help.

Now, where was I?

'Timbuctoo?'

'The boy Siddiq was sold and separated from his father—'

Shukran!

Adventure is an antidote to anguish. For Siddiq, the journey far north was so, in a caravan of three hundred camels, and more, which carried gum, and ivory from the dead as well as the ebony merchandise of the living. They travelled, swaying hypnotically atop the dromedaries, through lands which gauged the fire and shimmer of the days, lands of austere monoliths, ochre plains, chaoses of peaks, twisted rock, broiling blank blacknesses, sweeping dunes and rippled sand, and betwixt the swollen and crescent moons which tallied the ink and cut diamond skies of the Saharan nights. And he learnt words of an unfamiliar language: fad, tildechi, egredi—

'Ya Rahwun. I do not understand.'

'That is because our story-teller impresses us with his knowledge of the Tuareg language.'

Sahha. So perhaps our knowledgeable friend can translate as I write before me in the dust thus:

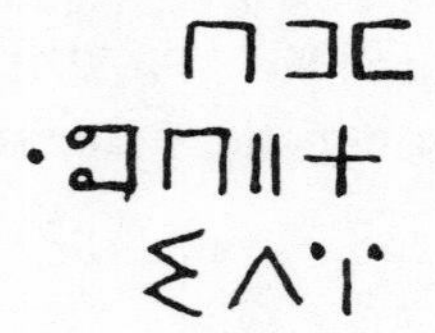

I am overwhelmed by the silence. Fad is thirst; tildechi is fatigue; egredi is sand. Oh! One other:

Akli: a black slave.

But I digress—

Reaching the M'Zab, the caravan continued, with a wary eye for bandits, up into the Atlas, to Medea. And as they neared this, the residence of the Bey of Tittery, Siddiq all but swooned, sure that the Trumpet must have sounded the Day of Reckoning, for this was surely Paradise! A sweet greenness of orchards and gardens bewitched the approach to the wall which was girdling the white city of soaring minarets and angled roofs, seemingly tethered to the world by the long stone ribbon of its aqueduct. But alas! the thought of reclining on soft couches and drinking the ginger-flavoured water from the Fount of Selsabil was premature, for it was this world, and there, a few days later, Siddiq was sold for two hundred boudjous cash, one hundred per cent profit to his captors. Salesmanship indeed: considering the boy's moonstruck convulsions, caused by itching the chilblains swollen and sore on his fingers and toes; bearing in mind that he had been popped into hysteria by the feathered spellcraft of the Devil, the flakes of snow which had trembled from a gunmetal sky.

Now Siddiq's buyer's name was Ibn Abdun, a Moor with origins in Andalus. Ibn Abdun had hair glistening smooth and black, and an aquiline nose, above lips full and red as a rose and a chin dimpled with a silver well, and his prosperity was told by the languor of his eyes, and a walk which was poised and grave. And riding a noble horse, north-westwards this master went with his slave, through forests of olive trees and trails of brushwood silvered with ice to descend a knife-edge trail along the chill, straight pass of the Chiffa, ever echoing with the scream of monkeys and torrents of water raging at the base of its sunless ravines. Then the plain of the Mitidja yawned wide ahead with an easy stretch of arms in surrender to the sky, but it was some distance on before Siddiq plucked courage and turned to see from whence they had come, and the wild and sombre blues of the Lesser Atlas reflected his heart, for the chain of rock deterred any last hope of return. And 'Ya-llah!' his master bade him hurry, and they skirted marshy land and hamlets ringed with Barbary figs, and leaving the flatland they climbed again and trod difficult paths until laurel trees and groves of palms marked the valley town of Kolea, a mere twelve leagues from their destination.

And so it was, after this further journey, that man and boy sighted Algiers, our beloved Mozghranna, call it as you will, and the tessellation of houses cascaded far before them in a dazzle of white to a lazuli sea. O, how Siddiq's almond-shaped eyes opened wide at the sight of that mysterious and impalpable water, the sea! Arriving at last at the city wall, master and servant were greeted by grins of welcome, from three human heads skewered on poles, which hurried them through al-Bab Azoun, where a cobra hissed and spired to the moan of a Moroccan snake charmer's pipe. Siddiq's bare feet throbbed, massaged by the rounded irregular stones which paved the street of the lower part of the city, Al Outha. Colours and costumes flooded around them: tawny burnouses, muslin or cashmere turbans, some wound around red fezzes, floating white cloaks and veils, gold, silver, and embroidered silks of belts, waistcoats, and kaftans, grey tunics sashed with blue, flaxen, peach, and pink full-sleeved gauze shirts over voluminous trousers, scarlet slippers, and yellow, white, and blue babouches. The air was swollen and restless with the lilt of language, of Arabic, of Berber, of Turkish, Hebrew, Italian, and Spanish. And in each breath a smell, seductive or repugnant, of attar of roses, of jasmine, of coffee, of spices and warm fresh bread, of man, of animals live and butchered, of urine, dung, vegetable peelings and other leavings. They jostled and wound on through the bazaar, passed a barber shaving a child's head, passed pots of make-up, blue for the eyebrows, red for the cheeks, yellow for the nails, passed stalls of coral beads and bracelets of plaited silk, and the gleam of brass and silver metalwork.

The crowded streets melted away as they made towards the upper part of Algiers, al-Jabal, ascending through a deep labyrinth edged by plain and windowless walls, and tunnelled fitfully by upper storeys propped on rows of tilted cantilevers. A twist, a turn, and from a cul-de-sac the bare breadth of two men, the rise of a few uneven steps gave to the inside of the house, which opened to the pearliness of a marble-floored courtyard set with the curve and verdure of an orange tree, and centred with an octagon of water reflecting the hyacinth-hued fall of the day.

Ibn Abdun lived with his wife, two sisters and his seven young children on the first floor of the house. The rooms were faced with picturesque blue and white Dutch tiles and tiles bold-patterned by the subtleties of symmetry, here and there set with bricks bearing varnished inscriptions of the Holy Qur'an. Elsewhere, the walls were hung with faded flags and elaborate draperies. Carpets from Rabat overlaid the floor with the floridness of spring. The carved wood ceilings were honeyed with gilt. Above this was a terrace with a view to the bay, and to the leaf-green slopes which faded and shaded into the rock ridge of the Djurdjura which trimmed the canopy of the sky.

Siddiq lived there with three other slaves on the ground floor. He swept and polished, he fetched and carried. He mashed together the leaves, seeds and flowers of hemp into a paste for smoking. He was submitted to the rigours of playing with Ibn Abdun's children, to the capriciousness of his mother, and the jackboot of his wife. At times he felt suffocated, but it was by none of this. He felt imprisoned by the city which shut fast its five gates at night, and shackled by its twines of streets. Only from the heights of the roof terrace could he breathe the lusciousness of liberation, momentarily cut adrift by the glinting sword edge of the Mediterranean horizon.

So Siddiq matured prematurely to manhood. And it was,

in those times of yore, on the eve of a Friday, that Muslim saints filled the Mosque of Sidi ar-Rahman in Algiers, and they voyaged from all the corners of the world, from Haf to Qaf. And the holy men entered the mosque from its dazzling depths, some in the guise of lions and leopards, and some as eagles and white doves whose spiralled downward flight metamorphosed them into Man. And when the saints were all assembled, sat on rugs in solemn posture, a sumptuous litter descended from the heavens bearing the King of Saints, and he began: 'O Saints of Allah! What advice will you offer me? Injustice is unleashed everywhere. Murders can no longer be counted. This one devours the property of that one. Everyone steals, weapons clutched in their hands, or through stealth. Judges are massacred for applying the law. People insult each other and fight. Anarchy abounds. And I ask you: what people will substitute itself for this decrepit domination? I have travelled through Allah's Empire in search of an answer, and have found none.'

The patron saint of Algiers rose. Said he, 'The Turk has betrayed the trust we placed in him, and will never enjoy more than a precarious authority. These domains are to be an appendage of France, and the fate of this land is in the hands of He who initiated the movement of the Celestial Bodies.'

So it was that the assembly adjourned to consider this, and consult Fate through their various devices. As you will know, the minor saints use sorcery and magic or simpler means, and so it was that the marabout Si Abd Allah brought together one white ox and one black ox, and muttered in their ears, at which the oxen butted heads in a fearsome fight and the white ox was defeated. Whereupon Si Abd Allah was satisfied, for he had determined that the white ox represented the white of the burnous, whilst the black ox symbolized the navy greatcoat of the French. And meanwhile the great saints read from the Sacred Tablet which stretched down from the throne of Allah to Earth, and on which was written for all Eternity what has been and what will be. God is blessed indeed!

And so the important saints of the Maghreb regathered to discuss the question of domination by France, and I give you a summary of the matters raised in the One Hundred and One Sessions.

It was said: the worshipper of church bells resembles a mosquito which pricks without pain but leaves a burning trace that becomes a pimple and a disease.

In Session 12 it was said that these worshippers of idols would come and implant themselves like grubs in meat. It was said that the infidel would redesign our statutes, and that he was of a changing race much like the chameleon who can assume seven colours.

In Session 18 it was asked: he is as sweet as a small lamb? Believe it, for he'll whip you like milk in a baked clay churn.

In Session 67 it was said that gold will become common, but the faith rare; cafés would be full but the mosques empty.

And worse, in Session 76, it was said that the Christians would encroach on our character bit by bit and many Muslims would be assimilated and adopt their manners and customs. At their schools they would learn to eat on high tables, to drink out of glasses with a napkin on their knees, all this with uncovered heads. Moreover, they would eat the meat of animals slaughtered in the Christian fashion. And Muslim women would follow the varying clothing fashions, and also grind their teeth and ogle like the French women do. And the true believers would watch on, their hearts secretly burning and saying: when will a Muslim government come to extinguish this fire that consumes us?

In Sessions 80 and 81 it was said: the infidels would flood us with their merchandise. The sugar they sold would be bleached with the bones of impure animals. The candles that we offer to our marabouts would contain pork fat mixed with the wax. The soap they would sell would be adulterated and our clothes would be washed with the residues of unclean animals. There would be left for us neither the state of purity nor worthwhile prayers.

Now, correct me, but did not Ibn Khaldun, good Berber that he was, write in *The Muqaddimah* that 'Places that succumb to Arabs are quickly ruined'? So it was that the Council of Saints compared Turkish society to the disease-ridden swamps of the Mitidja plains of that epoch. Quoth they: 'The Kingdom is like a muddy pool. Its waters will not clear as long as the Turks rule over us. We must make this swamp healthy by tearing despotism up by the roots. We need France. Wa-llah! Better the infidel than such tyranny. Let him come and administer, and reign and hold our cities. He shall move with soldiers as numerous as swarms of grasshoppers and with an energetic government establish the order that the Muslim kings of old could never achieve.'

In Session 17 it was said: they would manufacture a thingumabob which will remind us of our demons. This jinn would jig from one city to another whilst ringing its iron plates and hooked chains. Never was such a thing invented by Nimrud Ibn Kanʿan (the Kings who ruled all the earth). Starting up it would make the din of an ogress and with its whistle you would think you are hearing the howling of Satan. And what buildings they would build, as high as man could conceive and scraping the sky. O and how powerful and bright is the light which will light their homes at night!

In Session 33 it was said that the unbeliever would teach us the art of building roads and bridges.

In Session 57 it was said that distances would be diminished, making it possible to perform salat idh-dhur in Algiers and then salat il-asha in Tizi-Ouzou. News sent out at sunrise would receive a reply by sunset, and wires would be stretched which would enable one friend to talk to a far-off friend without seeing each other.

In Session 73 it was said that they would adorn our country with fine cultivation from which we Muslims would profit. They would even out uneven soil. The Christians would cause fountains to shoot from the bowels of the earth to quench thirst, and be channelled to make desert regions green.

And lo! in Session 76 it was said that they would appoint doctors for men who become ill, and women doctors for women. They would prepare medicines that they would sell to the rich and give away to the poor. They would achieve improvements about which we had not the slightest idea. It was said that under this rule the jackal and lamb would wander freely in the countryside. And it was argued that they would defend our soul from sin and keep us from alcoholic beverages and licentiousness. Anyone who lost all restraint would see himself imprisoned, reprimanded and fined, forced in the end to come back to God. Amen!

And afterwards.

In Algiers, over the tap and rattle of draught-boards and the noise of the card games in the cafés, and in the steam-filled rooms of the baths, Siddiq listened to the prophecy of one Si Akradar which clacked and quavered from everyone's lips, viz. *the hosts of the Christians shall come from all sides, and the mountains and towns shall shrink from us. They will cross over the sea and come from all quarters, horsemen and on foot. They will descend with an army like a raging fire, like a flying flash. They will arrive like a torrent in the dark night, like a cloud of sand driven before the wind. The churches of the Christians shall be raised. And the Christian expedition will smite Algiers and spread themselves abroad from there. They will rule over the Arabs according as God shall will and ordain. And everywhere all inhabited places shall be in anguish, from the east to the west.*

'A few more douros for our story-teller! His voice has vanished!'

'Do not delve into your pockets so fast. Ya Rahwun! First give us the answer to your riddle. The green slave bearing white children which turn black?'

Easy: an olive tree, that is the word of the puzzle. Is that a one-dinar coin? Sahha!

Suddenly I feel able to continue, so much so that I can leap the centuries to nearly the present, and stride the continents to Paris. That glorious city, Paris.

But brothers, remember the intuitive heart knows that glory is founded on mendacity.

There was . . . there was not. An open refrigerator in the city's suburbs gilded the well-wiped surfaces of a cramped kitchen as a young Algerian poured himself a glass of milk. Azallah Boudjemaa was twenty-six and his curse was an ulcer. And it happened that a year ago he had been to consult Monsieur le docteur, the straw-haired, cherry-lipped young graduate who thought himself the cat's miaow with his white coat and his stethoscope. He had diagnosed Azallah with a glance and, as a point of etiquette, a prod, two questions and a witty remark. He had tut-tutted, and suddenly serious, told Azallah to stop smoking and not to eat so much spiced food, especially harissa. Then he had leant back in his leather upholstered chair, studying his cuticles with a coy smile.

Next!

Now Azallah had never smoked (discounting the odd illicit Gitane of former school days); it was rare that he ate spiced food, and he loathed the red-hot paste, harissa. Hence his stomach had raged as he had returned home to the slab block where he lived in Courtillières, banged the front door and snapped at his startled mother, Nadia, for tearing parsley into a saucepan of chorba.

The fridge door clanked shut. The cold milk blanketed his stomach. He rubbed around the inside of the glass as he rinsed it under a tap, and set it on the drainer. There was a clatter as he accidentally knocked a pot into the sink. Whereupon the sound of steel container against steel container in the semi-darkness touched off a memory of a jangling illusive carillon in another continent . . . *dit-dit-dit dah-dah.*

In the living room, from the adjacent flat, came the yip yap yap of the Garniers' pooch. Azallah clicked on the television, volume loud. His father had bought the television six years ago, but wa-llahi! One of the first programmes watched had revealed that they were amongst the fifty-three per cent of Algerian families and single workers in France who owned one. Only twenty-seven per cent possessed a vacuum cleaner, and thirty-two per cent a car. The former was the easier club to join but, apart from being plugged in and performing for guests, the droning serpent had lain lifeless behind the settee, whilst Nadia still pointedly brushed away the dust with a broom. But then she had claimed the television an aquarium of the miniature and disembodied all conjured up by Satan, until seeing that in Algeria broadcasting always opened with a recitation from the Holy Qur'an.

Azallah stretched along the liver-coloured settee, and propped his head on one of the cream antimacassars which jacketed its arms. What was the channel? No matter! A camera panned politely over the concrete of the Parisian suburb Genevilliers. The lens weaved up a staircase, showing the graffiti which titivated the walls: *Marie C. is on the pill*; No to unemployment; a spray-painted penis hung with tufty testicles. And all the while a woman's voice scratched over the monochrome images.

'. . . and do you see those children playing on the stairs, tapping on the doors to amuse themselves? They're immigrants. Arabs. The noise! Always noise. Do you hear that? That's their music: drink a bottle of bleach and play a squeaky fiddle and there you have it. Ah monsieur! Their carpets hang over the balcony, winter and summer, day and night. And if I don't have carpets, I have Niagara Falls! Buckets of water over my clean washing without so much as a how do you do. And another thing: no pets are allowed. But I've seen sheep, I've *heard* sheep as they cut their throats. They say it's religious; I say it's pagan. *Pagan*. The noise! The blood! My washing! C'est la petite guerre quoi! And do you know what one of them said the other day? "Madame, I am as French as you are." With a name like Malika? I ask you. But then monsieur thinks I'm racist, non? Well I can live with the Portuguese, no problem with that. They're all Catholics. Like us. There'll be ten million Muslims in France by the end of the century. That's what my husband says. No birth control these Arabs, that's their trouble. Just Mecca Roulette. And there'll be the Qur'an and mosques everywhere, but no wine anywhere. And no cognac. And pork, no pork! Monsieur, what will France do without her hams and andouillettes? Where will I go to Mass? It's . . . it's . . . it's insupportable.'

Azallah crunched a piece of fingernail, and switched the television off.

Yip yap yap.

Such sentiments were on the increase. Trapped by the economic recession, the government of France had made every effort to seduce its quicksilver public, with champagne charm and vital statistics, pinpointing migrant workers as the cause of high unemployment amongst French nationals.

Thereupon *Le Monde* had reported that there was scarcely any evidence that a reduction in foreign workers would free an equivalent amount of jobs for the French.

Lies buzz like flies, but the truth has the brilliance of the sun!

And lo! Sometimes at night, as the twin dots of a digital clock flashed silent seconds into the shadows of the bedroom he had shared with his father, Azallah had pondered on his future. Recurrently in his dreams he was an acrobat, his white kit splendid against his olive skin, ever somersaulting from one trapeze to the other, to and fro in the dizzy heights of the big top, with sweat-wet unchalked hands, and no net below.

Then, last year, 1400 or 1980 as you will, a thunderhead moved across the skies of his life and boomed a fanfaronade in Algiers as a series of accords were signed with France, designed to encourage the voluntary return and assist the reinsertion of families into our economy and society. You will remember the shower of trinkets from which to choose: the repatriation allowance of four months' salary; the retraining programmes; or the loans to set up a small business.

Now in France, some of the Algerian community rejoiced. Many thought it not enough. A few sneered.

Azallah hesitated: his residence permit was coming up for renewal. Moreover, his father Mustafa, allah irahmu!, had been recently buried in the Kingdom of Saudi Arabia, having collapsed with sunstroke on the Plain of Arafat, whilst standing in prayer and glorifying God during that cornerstone of the pilgrimage to Mecca, the wuquf. This, I add, was a matter of open admiration and secret envy amongst certain of his friends and family, for do not forget, death during the Hadj ensures us the rewards of Paradise.

But the life cycle goes on and on and the birth of a son, to the elder of Azallah's sisters, had determined a vocation for their widowed mother, and thus Nadia had left Paris to live in Lyon, chez daughter, grandchild and Tunisian son-in-law, above their popular tiny restaurant (*le brik à l'oeuf* a speciality).

So, alone in the flat, he had but a single thing to contemplate: as he had returned to Algeria only once during his fourteen years in France, should he visit to see if he would relish living there now?

And all the while a proverb of his grandfather, Hadj Ali, echoed as mellow as his voice in his mind: there is no messenger like money.

Eight—

'—that's right, ya Rahwun! My brother in Paris shares accommodation. Eight in four bunks in two rooms, in a hostel in Chevilly. No shower. Communal cooking facilities. He leaves for work at five in the morning and returns after seven at night. He tries to study. He's been looking for a flat, or a room, but the reply has been the same: no North Africans. Yet Azallah Boudjemaa lives in a flat alone. Ya saʿdi!'

I suspect a trick to make me reveal whether or not Azallah quits France for good. Ya sidi, you can rest assured that if he does he'll immediately get in touch with your brother. But I must press on as the sun is reaching its zenith.

'Inshallah.'

1830. More than a date, more than a series of numbers, one eight three zero. It is the symbol branded by the white-hot iron which sizzled into the flesh of our history.

1830. It was a time when a pedigree of vain attempts by Charles X of France to reconcile the Crown with the democratic spirit of the Nation failed, and to blush unseen needed some glorious distraction . . . and hence the Flywhisk swished in His Highness' memory to gather the first capful of wind to billow the sails of a naval fleet from Toulon, cannons primed and bound for Algiers.

My mind reels, and I recollect the prophecy of Si Akradar.

At the peninsula of Sidi Ferrudj, three thousand seven hundred troops landed on 14 June to advance thirty kilometres east to Algiers.

And ladies, elegant with their piled hair, bonnets, long dresses and parasols, gaped and gasped, from the cushioned comfort of pleasure boats, at the naval bombardment of North Africa's white pyramid-city.

Memories beat like cymbals on my brain, and my thoughts resound with the words of Si Akradar. *They will cross over the sea and come from all quarters, horsemen and on foot.*

At the beginning of summer, beneath a sapphire sky, the white flag sewn with the gold fleur-de-lis was hauled high above the city, ending three centuries of Turkish domination.

(It was not enough: four weeks later, Charles X was forced to abdicate and flee to England and the unfurled bars of the tricolour replaced the flapping fleur-de-lis.)

Meanwhile the Convention of the 4th of July had guaranteed the liberty of the vanquished population, of whatever class. It guaranteed their religion. It guaranteed their property. And it guaranteed their commerce and their industry.

The relief was palpable. For across the years many families such as Ibn Abdun's had acquired assets in Algiers, for the most part shops and fondouks, and secured them in a pious trust, legally known as the *habus*. Some endowed money for the maintenance of mosques; some supported primary and secondary schools, the m'sid for learning to read and write the Holy Qur'an and the madrasa for the studies of grammar, metaphysics, theology, arithmetic and law; and some benefited the Foundation of Mecca and Medina which gave donations to the poor and assistance to those intent on performing the pilgrimage. Likewise, other properties bequeathed a comfortable private income . . . and still would do so, it seemed, in perpetuity.

Yes: a city's fears were balmed by zephyrs of sighs.

Had they not heard . . . ?

During the fire-hot days and deep velvet nights, the notables of Algiers, Ibn Abdun amongst them, talked of little but, even congratulated themselves on, the splendent saffron dawn of a new era.

Were they not haunted by . . . ?

Approaching us from the far distance is the paradiddle of a French military drum. Listen!

Listen, like no one listened to . . .

. . . the prophecy of Si Akradar. O as the poet has said in these extempore verses:

Your defenders have betrayed you,
Without doubt they were drunk.
Tears gush from my eyes,
And my heart is oppressed by sobs.
Mozghranna, who will heal your wounds?

By the end of the year a decree had allowed the demolition of property in the city for the purpose of the public good. By the end of the year . . . a decree had ordered all habus property to be confiscated – the majority of houses and commercial property in Algiers.

It took just that: a spiky copperplate of alien characters, in a language queerly written from left to right. Just that, just ink on paper, and Ibn Abdun lost most of his revenues as his property was snatched or demolished, and left only with a leather pouch feather-light with compensation.

So buildings began to crash in al-Bab Azoun, al-Bab al-Wadi and around Jamiʿ al-Kabir, looked on by the ousted and the dispossessed. Lunation followed lunation: the city rumbled like a volcano, thousands of its citizens the cinders and lava that sputtered and flowed down and away on the waves of the sea, or along the roads into the countryside or east to Qusantina, bundled possessions carried in hands, on backs, on donkeys and on mules.

In two years mathematics could not comprehend the number of houses demolished, cleared for the oblong, tree-planted Place du Gouvernement, and for the wide streets trimmed with four-storey white buildings, their frilled façades buxom with balconies, spangled with windows, and lace-hemmed with arcades. And where do I begin counting the mosques transfigured into Christian churches and chapels?

O Mozghranna, who will heal your wounds?

And know, O brothers, that despite all the juggling shows and fandangle of nineteenth-century French civilization, Ibn Abdun was irritable and off-hand! Could he not laugh at the Frenchmen, the people who crushed themselves into innumerable clothes just as the dwarf palm tightens its footing in its woody envelopes? The people who could not take even a step without turning and turning again? Alas! Siddiq watched him turn sallow of complexion. He saw him neglect his prayers and lose his appetite and waste to bone. And at nightfall Ibn Abdun would pace, restlessly, relentlessly through the house, unable to sleep, and once, when the courtyard was feverish with moonlight, he crouched and retched, half-choking half-sobbing, into its pool, momentarily disfiguring the clear water and the mirrored scimitar of silver therein.

One morning there was a scream, and the wife of Ibn Abdun all but tumbled down the narrow winding staircase from the upper floor, then sallied forth with unusual energy into the kitchen. She folded her arms across the tight silk bodice beneath her sequinned négligé, tucked her chins into her neck, and narrowed her eyes.

Said she: 'Four gold bracelets, two rings and my favourite anklet have disappeared in the night.'

The wife of Ibn Abdun was a big woman. Siddiq and a second slave cowered; a third began to cry.

Said she: 'Stop that snivelling and search the house!'

Ibn Abdun paced into the room.

Said he: 'The jewellery will be found by sunset, inshallah!' And he smacked Siddiq across the head.

The act stunned them all. But there was no time to be wasted, and the children at least were gleeful as the house was turned upside down and pulled inside out.

Meanwhile, there was food to buy on a sou, and Siddiq

was sent to the bazaar to haggle over now ever-rising prices. And it was there that Siddiq espied his master accost the Della a-strutting about laden with burnouses, ringed fingers clutched round bracelets and other bijouterie. Siddiq gazed, truly dazed, as Ibn Abdun passed four gold bracelets and two rings to the man. Coins exchanged hands. Then Ibn Abdun was gone.

Whereupon Siddiq hastened after his master, dropping a bunch of coriander in mid-negotiation, dodging an oil carrier with goat-skin pitchers, winding through the maze of people. In a dead-end alleyway Ibn Abdun rapped twice, and twice again on a door. It opened a fraction, then barely more to let him in. Siddiq waited until the noon sun had chased all the shadows from the narrow lane. He then too rapped twice, and twice again on the door. Inside mats lined the floor, and upon them men reclined with opium pipes. Siddiq crouched beside his master. His face was flushed and he looked back at his slave with excited eyes and laughed a vacant laugh.

Outside Siddiq returned, and waited to steer Ibn Abdun back to his house. In the obscurity of the night-time street, they passed ghostly images cast by the bob of yellow flame, as a procession of lantern bearers guided a bride to the wedding feast at the bridegroom's home.

Allah is All-knowing!

I've something to tell you. Only seventeen years after the French landed at Sidi Ferrudj, that open-minded and liberal historian, Alexis de Tocqueville, put pen to paper appalled by the wanton destruction of our towns and property by the colonial administration. And with respect to habus property, his quill nib rasped: *Everywhere we have put our hands on these revenues, we have ruined charitable institutions, dropped the schools and dispersed the seminaries. Around us lights have been extinguished, and the recruitment of men of religion and men of law has ceased. In other words we have rendered Muslim society much more miserable, disorganized, ignorant and barbaric than it was before knowing us.*

All inhabited places shall be in anguish . . .

Do you remember the prophecy of Si Akradar?

The métro pulled into Châtelet. A young woman stepped in. She seated herself precisely opposite Azallah Boudjemaa. The lustre of her face outshone the bright full moon and her eyes resembled the eyes of gazelles, her lips were as coral, and her hair was as flaxen as honey, and gathered and teased by clear-varnished finger tips into a pony tail. The cut of her coat was softened by a mist of perfume, and her feet were bred into low-heeled calf-skin shoes. The warning siren sounded, the doors slid shut, and the train accelerated into tunnel blackness and windows became mirrors.

The métro pulled into Hôtel de Ville. People milled, they exited and entered. The siren like a mule braying, the rush into darkness. Azallah glanced at her. His mouth felt dry. He tried to swallow. She was so . . . unattainable.

The métro pulled into St Paul. He wished she would get off. She looked across at him. He loosely clenched his fists to hide his bitten nails. She smiled. Wa-llahi! She smiled. At the thousand raven curls and the blue O so gentle eyes and the fine nose and at the cruel grace of his mouth, and her gesture winged him to the frontier of another world but where, monsieur, was the valid passport and visa? He stared down at his lap. He could have leant over and asked: 'How about dinner? Or a drink?' He didn't mind that she would refuse, what he minded was how.

The métro pulled into Bastille. At nineteen, Azallah had asked out the shop girl, Josette, at the pâtisserie where he worked. For weeks she had flirted with him, flirted until he was lantern-jawed and overcome with delirium. So he bought her red roses and asked her out and had she simpered or did she purr? Hayhalati! *Grrrrr*, she had snarled, *va te faire foutre, sale bicot*. And the profusion of scarlet petals was left to shrivel in its gown of cellophane. Now opposite, the young woman uncrossed her ankles and stood. She was alighting at the Gare de Lyon. Azallah was uneasy. Maybe she would think that he was following her: perhaps she wanted him to follow her?

The métro pulled into the Gare de Lyon. She threw up the handle and the door opened with a bleat. Azallah followed her out, a bag in one hand, and fingering his yellow ticket with the other. He sat down on one of the platform's scooped seats. The train had gone. She . . . had gone.

He walked up the stairs and through the tiled tunnel. The air resonated all around him with the melancholy of a cello played with some passion by a lily-faced, cashmere-jumpered, teenage musician. Beside him the red felt base of his open instrument case was gaudy with coins of silver and bronze. Azallah grinned, and tossed in one Algerian dinar.

At the junction with various exits, leading up to the station or on and out to Boulevard Diderot, stood a shop, its counters opulent and musk-scented with fruit. The vendor was Arab, and for a second both he and Azallah dithered, tongue-tied by propriety.

Said he, the vendor: 'Is-salamu ʿalay-kum.'

Said he, Azallah: 'Wa ʿalay-kum is-salam.'

Said he, the vendor: 'Monsieur?'

O the diplomacy of language, my friends!

Said he, Azallah: 'Un kilo de pommes et un kilo d'oranges, s'il vous plaît.'

Said he, the vendor: 'Wahid kilu mawz wa wahid kilu sina?'

Said he, Azallah: 'Na'am.'

O the diplomacy of language!

The man gathered the fruit into two brown-paper bags.

Said he, the vendor: 'Ha huwwa! Ça fait dix-huit francs.'

Said he, Azallah: 'Shukran.'

Said he, the vendor: 'Afwan.'

Gambling on a gesture or look. Threading through a scorpion's nest of etiquette, assumptions, and education and choice. O the diplomacy of language, the diplomacy of language. Enough!

Azallah continued up the escalator to the concourse and bought a second-class ticket for the 20:42 train to Marseille. He strolled outside, the majestic façade and clocktower of the station floodlit behind him, the kaleidoscopic dash of neons in front. He crossed to the corner café, the *Européen*, which was filling with customers sitting and settling around starched white tablecloths attended by waiters in white jackets and black bow-ties. A chef was arranging the pinks and greys of seafood on a counter of crushed ice which glittered like the restaurant it fronted. White, yellow, and red car lights dazzled the night. Azallah strolled aimlessly, bag in hand, down the Rue de Lyon, pausing to see the furniture, leather settees and marble-topped tables, in the windows of Roche Bobois. He read the prices in terms of fractions and multiples of his weekly wage. He crossed over the road, whereupon he turned back. A woman, her cheeks rashed with rouge, and her hair tangerine, posed in vixen boots and fish-net stockings at the corner of a narrow street, and chafed her hands against the winter night. Azallah passed the vestibule of a three-star hotel; he passed a delicatessen, closing, taking oblong baskets of vegetables from the pavement to an interior gleaming with shelves of wine and waxen with an array of cheeses. Then, reaching the Gare de—

'—why by train?'

What?

'It's speedier, more glamorous, even cheaper, by aeroplane.'

Naʿam: from the airport at Orly Sud, Algeria is a mere two hours, above the clouds, to the steady lullaby drone of engines. But it is a journey without ritual, and far too fast to unscramble emotions. The Gare de Lyon is a temple built to the spirit of an industrial age, the rail-head of a century of our wretchedness. It is chilled with the ghosts of tens of thousands and more who had left for a new life in Algeria, and of impoverished Algerians seeking a better life in France. As evanescent as the smoke and vapour of past decades of steam trains, it swirls with the phantoms of Algerian soldiers and workers supplied to the Metropole during the Great War. Its walls still echo with the footsteps of the cheap labour which fuelled France's economic recovery and reconstruction after its liberation from Nazi occupation by the Allies. Its air is still pungent with the bitterness of those fleeing our Independence twenty-five years ago. The glass and metal roof hugs all these countless departures and arrivals, man-made flesh and bones over the haemorrhage which has been the destiny spattering each and every one of our fortunes. Thus it was, on these platforms, that Azallah Boudjemaa, aged twelve, had first set foot in Paris with his family. It was thus that it was here, O my brothers, that Azallah began the journey to Algeria.

In the carriage he ignored an empty compartment, choosing one already occupied by a priest and an elderly woman. Whereupon the train jerked, relaxed and rattled out of the station, rain ran in rivulets down the window, and spells of blackness reflected life as a fantasy faced by glass.

And so I must take my leave, and in doing so I give you this riddle to guess:

> The hare is in the forest, and the saluki is near by;
> The hare does not move, and the saluki does not eat it.

I'll give you the answer next week, if the incentive is enough for me to return . . .

Shukran . . . Shukran!

Praise be to God, the One, the Creator, the Maker!

The Second

Yesterday I went to the hospital at Biskra. Nearly four hours by bus. There and back. Oh, one of you says rather sternly I should give up smoking! Well, I went with my aged father: it's he that is ill, not me.

We began to queue at five in the morning, after salat al-fajr. Nor were we the first!

Yet people who arrived well after us were shown straight in, or became next in line. A name was dropped here, a few dinar exchanged hands there. Well, my blood pressure was rising, so I counted my loose change in the event that something vital burst and I required emergency treatment. Then, al-hamdu li-llah! We were shown to the doctor. O my brothers, did you know that there are almost as many foreign doctors in Algeria as Algerian doctors? A souvenir of colonial education. But there was a surprise in store: our doctor wasn't Russian, but Asian. His French, at least, was original. I gave him the note from our clinic here. He opened it solemnly, and then asked me to translate it as it was written in Arabic. I braced myself for the worst, and took the letter. Its considered opinion was that my father should have a check-up in the manner of I know-not-what. So I became the interpreter whilst the doctor asked questions about my father's symptoms. Now and again he shouted a hearty *inshallah* at my father to relax things a little. Consequently my father became reticent about the pains he had been having. I reminded him that he had been losing weight, but to that he pooh-poohed. I lost my patience, whereupon my father claimed to feel much improved, and wished to go to a mosque for salat idh-dhur. I thanked the doctor and we left.

On the journey back I was in a tizz about the waste of the day. I blamed the wait in the hospital and my aged father's awkwardness on the blackness of my mood. For had we not voted for a constitution ten years ago in our glorious *Charte Nationale* which guaranteed that the State would protect the health of we citizens and assure a public health service which was free? I remember nothing about luck or string-pulling but there was the phrase: 'public health must contribute to the promotion of man to prepare for progress in a thrilling and socio-cultural world in perpetual transformation'. I mentioned to my father about reading the small print.

Said he: 'My son, this is a young nation. You must be patient.'

Hhm. Hhemmm! Huum!

Na'am. I should give up smoking.

'Ya Rahwun. The solution of the hare and the saluki. One or both must have perished, so the riddle is Death.'

Wrong!

'Has it blood or not?'

Judge for yourself, for the answer is Algiers and the Sea.

In the name of Allah, the Compassionate, the Merciful!

And it was there in Mozghranna in ancient times, that Ibn Abdun set me an example: he stopped smoking . . . opium. With Siddiq ever at his side, wiping away the rushes of cold sweat, he conquered the spasms and pains voyaging through his body and which hacked and cut his stomach with a pair of ragged-bladed scissors.

And lo! Shortly afterwards, Siddiq reached his twentieth year, and was summoned in the freshness of a summer evening to the roof terrace of the house where Ibn Abdun contemplated the twilight sea and its thousand scintillations.

Said he, Ibn Abdun: 'Ya Siddiq! It is customary that after nine years as a slave you be given your liberty.

'Now, as you are aware, half of the citizens of Algiers have left in the last six years, and I am making arrangements to move to Fez. If you were to remain with me, I would count it as an honour, for you have served my family well. In the mean time, I give you this purse of gold, and beg that you acquit me of responsibility.'

Twenty-year-old Siddiq swayed a little, his body as lithe as a corn-stalk in the breeze. For a moment he was silent and he beheld the faintness of the crescent moon and a first star in the deepening sky.

Said he, Siddiq: 'May God acquit you of responsibility, O master, and I thank you for your offer. But in my waking hours and in the fathoms of my dreams, I wonder whether I should return south to where I spent the first years of my life?'

Said he, Ibn Abdun: 'Then my advice to you is to heed this proverb: take the counsel of one greater and one lesser than yourself, and afterwards form your own opinion.'

And so it was that Siddiq posed his problem to the Imam of the mosque of Jamiʿ al-Jadid, for he was a learned man acquainted with all languages and characters.

Said he, the Imam: 'The journey south will be perilous, and the life there will be hard. You might fall prey to another razzia, be recaptured, and resold as a slave. But in Algiers there is the possibility for a comfortable life, and there are many opportunities to find employment amongst your brother Muslims, or even the infidels. Ruhul ʿali-khyr ya-sidi!'

Presently, Siddiq asked the opinion of the youngest slave-girl in the household of Ibn Abdun.

Said she: 'Take the money and return to your village. Marry and have children, and tell them of the youth that you have spent.'

And she talked this sort of talk for a while.

Thereupon life had become difficult, and Siddiq was in a state of confusion, perplexed in his mind, until, lo! he explained his dilemma to another free slave in his ken.

Said he: 'Ya Siddiq! It is nearing the start of Ramadan, whence begins the forty days in which you can undertake the ceremony of the jalab where the Devil will enter you and allow you to foresee the Future.'

And when Siddiq heard this, his muscles quivered, his teeth chattered, his spittle dried up and he became blind about what to do, but it was thus that he went to consult the Chief of the Negroes in Algiers, the venerable Kait-laus-fan, and told him of his wish for prevision. Accordingly the jalab was set for the seventh night after the sighting of the full moon which marked the start of Ramadan.

At the appointed time, Siddiq was shown into a room concealed by a brocade curtain, and furnished with silken stuffs gold-starred, and spread with Constantinople carpets aplenty. In a court a knife was drawn several times around the throats of four white hens before their sacrifice, and Siddiq was startled to see a headless fowl run through the curtain and into the room, pursued by a young boy in a loin-cloth. Whereupon several black damsels, a delight of comeliness and perfect loveliness, entered the room and diffused censor-perfumes, and by the light of waxen candles undressed Siddiq and with their fingers anointed each of his joints with the still-warm chicken blood from a silver bowl. Then a potion of mastic, sandalwood and jasmine oil was massaged into his ebony skin, and a long embroidered kaftan was pulled over his head, and tied with a belt tasselled with tiny conch shells and coral beads which pattered like a rainstorm whenever Siddiq moved. And thus they waited.

And lo! at that moment in the first light of morning when a black thread could be told from a white thread, a group of thirty-three musicians entered with tambourines, dulcimers, pot-drums, fiddles and recorders. They threw down and unrolled a rug of the purest silk, a Persian hunting carpet from Kashan. Siddiq was led to its centre by the damsels. The music struck up, and he reeled with its rhythm. Then all at once he began to dance, performing whirls and pirouettes and there came forth from the carpet miniature leopards, lions, antelopes and wolves all darting and snarling and hurtling around him. Yet still he danced, his body writhing and repelling the tiny mouths and needle teeth which attacked him. Thereupon more small figures, turbanned horsemen armed with lances, swords and bows, galloped wing-footed in pursuit of the beasts all around him. And Siddiq toppled, downwards into the raging flames of a dragon's jaws . . .

'And then, ya Rahwun? And then?'

Wa-llahi! My mind is as empty as the circle in the sand before me.

'A few douros for our story-teller everybody!'

Sahha! Ah: miraculously my memory returns—

'Al-hamdu li-llah!'

. . . there was a roar like a tempest and Siddiq was soaring skywards through the air duct of a house hollowed into the bowels of the ground, and spired up a shaft which echoed with a century of voices. He was propelled on towards the edge of the celestial sky, and then tumbled spiralling amidst a blizzard of rose-pink blossom towards a frosted salt lake on a Persian-blue horizon. His dance became faster, more fantastic, and aflame with frenzy until he contorted and collapsed. The music clashed and screeched whilst the damsels shuffled towards him on their knees with reviving showers of scent from silver vessels. Thereupon the music became as dulcet as plashing water in a verdant oasis whilst Siddiq sprang back and forth in cartwheels diagonally across the carpet, until all at once he screamed, and crashed to the ground in a swoon. The onlookers whispered that Beelzebub had entered his being. And Siddiq saw before him a giant nest atop a precipice. He saw flights of birds and schools of fishes. Then the very room spun into a cyclone, and his chest heaved with a violence of spasms as he began to cough and to choke until he virtually expired.

And lo! Azallah Boudjemaa was seated in the train compartment wrapped in a semi-darkness folded with shadows and memories. There was the journey to Paris nearly fifteen years afore, and the view-as-a-child of his father, Mustafa, dressed in an awkward-fitting three-piece suit, his shirt buttoned to the collar, but no tie, his face swart with stubble and impassive but for one little blue vein pulsing in his temple. Opposite had sat Azallah's mother, Nadia, draped in a white haik which covered the tattoo on her forehead which marked the birth of her son and heir (but who had died in infancy). Her eyes burned with the knowledge that the arrival in Paris would be the start of a long battle against defeat. Azallah's two sisters, dressed in identical frilled dresses, their hair plaited and ribboned to impress Paris, slept entwined about each other like a knot of Arabic calligraphy. On the rack lay two new suitcases, bought and shown off with pomp to the family in Algiers, then packed beyond capacity, and one was now tied shut with string, the locks having burst during the turmoils of disembarkation and the douane at the port of Marseille.

Yellow light splashed through the carriage and drained away as instantly as water spilt on sand, and thereupon the darkening daubed a long-forgotten interior across the mind.

Home: a single-storey, windowless house, one third divided by a low wall giving to a lower level for their oxen and their cows. Above had been a loft where Azallah had slept with his brother, sisters and mother amongst the hay and the straw. In the main part of the house he could remember his father's and grandfather's rifles on the wall. Beneath them the loom. By the door water jars and baskets filled with dried figs and couscous. The flush of cinder in the dwelling's navel, a hollow fixed by three stones and set with cooking utensils. He recalled his mother bent on her knees, polishing the black clay-and-dung floor, the sounds of her breath answering to the sussurus from each spiral rub of the stone in her hand, truly seeming the most intimate of conversations. The house was a house organized by opposites: high and low; fire and water; day and night; cooked and raw; male and female; culture and nature. And as such it was to be the cradle of a life governed by dualism: Algeria and France; Muslim and Christian; Arabic and French; colonized and colonist; poor and rich; immigrant and emigrant.

The engine brakes began to screech the scream of a new-born child.

Now. Know that birth is the first rite of passage from darkness into light. Cut from Nadia with a knife, Azallah was swathed as he cried, in coarse bindings usually used for lashing sheaves, and he first suckled the tawny nipple of his mother's breast on the day that our nation was awakened in the manner that the poet Taibi hath said:

> Brother! Lift up your eyes to the blue sky of Algeria!
> And realize that a star is missing and that it must be
> put there tomorrow . . .
> Guerrilla!

Al-hamdu li-llah! It was the day that the FLN, the Front de Libération Nationale, launched its struggle for an independent Algeria, striking when France's morale was rock-bottom, recently defeated at Dien Bien Phu in Indo-China, and troubled with Moroccan and Tunisian nationalism already in the ascendant. It was the day that a handful of French and Algerian civilians and military were killed, the day that telegraph poles were felled, cork and tobacco stores fired, some bombs were exploded and others aborted, in seventy synchronized attacks.

O I said killed! I should have said martyred, for this day was All Saints' Day. Nineteen hundred and fifty-four anno Domini.

But France did not accept our invitation to negotiate peace and concede us our independence. No: France was not to be cowed.

The train had stopped at Dijon, and looking out, the dalliance and bustle along the bright-lit platform was soundless, seeming theatrical. Azallah watched a man urge a woman towards the train. She stepped back shaking her head. He tugged her sleeve. The train began to pull away, and the man's face darkened with anger and he strode off, leaving the woman and the suitcase behind. They grew smaller. The stage was replaced by night. Then the compartment door crashed open, and a young soldier entered, and he swung his bag up onto the rack, and removed his beret, and sat down facing Azallah.

Now this soldier, his face was as fresh as milk, as fresh-faced as the boy nearly a generation ago, who, raw in receipt of his baccalaureate and dreaming of the Sorbonne, had lingered, a glass of pastis so cool in his hand, in the cafés, among the breezes of conversation and light laughter which stirred beneath the plane trees, along the Cours Mirabeau in Aix-en-Provence. Wa-llah! It was the end of innocence and the requiem of one's control for, one mid-morning, just a few months later, that boy was the conscript who had gambolled like a lamb through the threshold and into the penumbra of a Kabylie home, his sub-machine-gun brandished like a handshake, his presence violating a world of intimacy and secrecy, and his voice spewing a language which slithered like a snake.

Then there was a hush.

'So it seems, ya Rahwun!'

I have mislaid my cigarettes. My nerves are too frayed to continue without one . . . A Gauloise! Sahha habib! Where was I?

'We were left with silence . . .'

Hmmm.

Thereupon, Nadia stood, from behind the loom, framed by the intruder's shadow.

Thereupon, her daughters ran round to her from the hand-mill.

Thereupon, six-year-old Moktar tried to grab the gun and three-and-a-half-year-old Azallah battered the soldier's thighs with his tiny fists.

And then there was a thud as the gun butt against Moktar's head, and the puncture of his skin, commenced the tattoo of *re-groupe-ment*. A word with an aftertaste as sour as an olive picked and eaten straight from a tree.

Not new to colonial Algeria, population regrouping had

allowed the expropriation of our most fertile lands a hundred-odd years ago and quashed resistance by breaking up tribal structures. The cash compensations? Bi–llah! What there was was soon squandered by the fellah, so unused was he to handling money, and presently many were forced to work as farm hands for wages or migrate on to the towns.

Not new to the French Army, population regrouping had been used in Indo-China to prevent the rural population from helping the communist partisans. People were torn from their homes, their villages razed to the ground, and vast areas became free-fire zones for ground and air forces. Stray into one, O my brothers, and you'll be the victim of some finger somewhere a-twitching on a trigger.

And so, population regrouping, under the trade mark of *regroupement*, its label assuring 'the fastest relief of irritation and the most effective means to pacification', was dusted from the military medicine chest, and prescribed as the ideal elixir vitae for colonial Algeria. To the rat-tat-tat of gunfire, regroupement was daily applied to affected areas, storming a balance sheet of eight thousand hamlets and villages burned or wrecked, and two million three hundred and fifty thousand people displaced, one third of the rural population, all by the time Azallah was not quite seven. A balance sheet, I add and which will you know, helped the FLN turn a quack military remedy into a political victory.

But what did Azallah's village know of the war? It knew that Nadia's brother, ever restless, had left to fight, safeguarded by verses from the Holy Qur'an folded and stitched into a deerskin pouch no larger than a date, and hung around his neck on a thong. And it knew of the leaflets which had floated lazily down from the sky, like shavings from the clouds, and commencing thus:

APPEAL TO THE MUSLIM POPULATION

Agitators, among them foreigners, have provoked bloody troubles in our country and have installed themselves notably in your region. They are living off your own resources . . .

SOON A TERRIFYING CALAMITY, FIRE FROM THE SKY, WILL CRASH DOWN ON THE HEADS OF THE REBELS.

After which the paix française will reign once more.

Whereupon . . .

Nothing.

Until . . . the day that Azallah's father left at daybreak, and saw a crippled fox, and rather than return to remake his going out, hurried on.

And soon after, Azallah's sisters wept and wailed as Nadia bent in silence over Moktar's still body. Azallah bit his lip, for the moment he was the man of the family.

Said she, Nadia: 'He's alive, al-hamdu li-llah! Calm yourselves and gather what you can. God is the best protector and He is the most merciful of the merciful.'

And Azallah squared his small shoulders, and they left their home, Moktar carried in his mother's arms, the girls half-lifting part-dragging untidy bundles, blankets, and clothes, and Azallah entrusted with the small woven bag fastened with a braid of loops which contained their Qur'an, brought from Mecca by his grandfather Hadj Ali, who had made the pilgrimage as a young man. The other precious things they could not take: whether the protector of the family honour, the main beam of the house; or the loom; or the umbilical cords of Azallah's sisters buried beneath it for the time now never to come, when each would have stepped deftly through the warp towards the wall to secure their virginity until marriage; or, or . . .

Outside, the village was in chaos, a muddle of braying donkeys, lowing cattle, barking dogs, bleating goats, baaing sheep and squawking chickens, screaming women and crying children, and overall the shouts of the militia. Standing a little apart were the older boys and the men, strangely quiet spectators of the scene. Buildings were doused with petrol. Lavender-lipped flames swallowed up the dwellings, whispering through the esparto-grass baskets, the mats, the chests and benches, the green fodder, the straw, the wool-strung looms, the grain, and the wooden lofts. Nadia turned away, only to see soldiers prance daintily to drape her wedding dress grotesquely across a tree, and a flask of water from the Meccan well of Zam-zam be smashed to smithereens. Then she and the villagers froze and looked to Hadj Ali as the main beam of his house gave a resounding crack, for it foretold the death of him, the head of the family.

Whereupon they were ordered to walk away, the vibrations from two exploding hand-grenades crystallizing a part of each and every soul. Azallah, his head resting on his grandfather's shoulder, glimpsed the conscript with a face no longer fresh, but crimson and crumpled from the hysteria and tears just checked by a slap from his commandant.

The villagers walked, a straggling line of people and their livestock, led and tailed by military jeeps. They walked, without food, through the foothills blazed with sulphur clouds of broom until at a crossroads they were separated; Azallah's grandfather and father and family were herded into one group, and his uncle and his family were rounded into another. And so other families were split asunder, and all the livestock was hastily divided. And on they trudged, into the poppy-red sky of a falling night, escorted towards a satanic brilliance of light, regroupement centre KM 17.

Ho, what bleary-eyed visions of a child! The watchtower

ahead had seemed a head upon a neck, and the stretch of pitched roofs like a jagged back. Azallah had clutched his grandfather's hand, and secretly wondered if they were all going to be fed to this creature, and would his throat be cut like a sheep to celebrate il῾id? And in a tiny voice he spake this terror.

Said he, Hadj Ali: 'Do hearts not become tranquil in remembering God?'

Then the complex took shape. A double gate was opened, but they were forced to leave their animals outwith the taut barbed-wire fences. And from the orders hurled at them from here, from there, and there and here, Azallah picked out the three words, *melons*, *ratons*, and *bicots*, derogatory slang which was the embryo of a new language.

Know, O brothers, that this was The Beginning, for as the poet hath said:

The day we had revealed the word 'bonsoir'
we received a blow to our chin,
we had been satisfied by imprisonment.

The day we had revealed 'bonjour'
we received a punch on our nose,
for us the blessings had stopped.

The day we had revealed 'merci'
we received a thump on our throat,
the sheep inspired more fear than us.

The day we had revealed 'cochon'
a dog valued honour better than us,
the share-cropper had bought a mule.

The day we had revealed 'frère'
we received a knock to our knee,
and we walked with shame in our breast.

The day we had revealed 'diable'
we had received a punch that rendered us stupid,
we had become carriers of dung.

They therefore proceeded into the compound, and one by one the families were ushered into an office where behind a wooden desk sat an officer, with a head as a dome, nostrils like ewers and a look which was lowering and fierce. From the ceiling the enigma of an electric bulb blazed like an earth-bound star from beneath its metal shade. Then through an Algerian interpreter, the officer started to take down their names.

Said he, the interpreter: 'Mustafa Boudjemaa, what is the name of your wife?'

And lo! the response was the rustle of a black moth frantic and flapping beneath the light shade. Azallah's father shifted uneasily where he stood, unwilling to dishonour himself by speaking the name of his wife in front of others, when even at home he would call Nadia with a gesture or the name of his eldest daughter.

Said he, the interpreter: 'Aywa?'

Said he, Mustafa: 'I cannot give you the name of the mother of my children.'

Said he, the interpreter: 'You must, ya sidi.'

Somewhere, in the near distance, a dog bayed.

Said he, Mustafa: 'I cannot give you her name.'

The officer looked up, impatience tensing in his face.

Said he, the officer: 'Et alors?'

The room was suddenly resonant with the shrill of crickets.

Said he, the interpreter: 'The name of his wife is Fatima.'

Thus far concerning them: and as regards another.

They recount that in olden times the marabout Si Abd Allah one day hazarded to pass through the coastal town of Tenes, whose inhabitants were such scoundrels that its reputation cannot be described by the tongue.

Now, these Tenesians, always full of disbelief, decided to test the piety of the marabout during his sojourn. They donned the garb of gladness, and decorated the markets and streets, and drums were beaten and pipes were sounded, and extraordinary dances were performed. And in the moon-tide they brought tables before him arranged with an abundance of food, viands and seafood, and sweetmeats and fruit and honey fritters, and in the centre-dish they served a cat, which had been stripped of its fur and tail, then basted on a spit, then set on a mound of couscous.

However, Si Abd Allah was too worthy a marabout not to notice what this meat actually was at a glance.

Cried he, the marabout Si Abd Allah: 'Sob!'

Now know that this interjection was used to chase away importunate cats, whereupon the roasted animal fled the plate like an arrow from a bow. And then the marabout threw at his hosts this apophthegm:

Tenes!
Town built on a manure-heap,
Its water is blood,
Its air is poison,
By God! Abd Allah does not sleep there.

So saying, he took up his brass-headed stick, and he went on his way. And to that I can only add: Amen!

And Azallah fared on also, with the blessing of Allah (whose name be exalted!). His companions in the train compartment were asleep, and saliva dribbled, like a snail trail of mucus, from the gaping mouth of the priest, and the old woman rent the air with horrible snores. Meanwhile, the young soldier had tumbled into the slumber of an angel. The time was 1:25. The train was due to arrive in Marseille at 5:15, but was running late. Here, I will acquaint thee with the fact that Azallah normally arose at five, which marked that empty hour when the immigrant worker in Paris is King. He began work at the pâtisserie at a quarter to six. Not thirteen minutes or fourteen minutes but fifteen minutes to six. Exactly.

Time is infinite, yet Man has tried to tame it by dividing it into hours, minutes and seconds. In the early years of Azallah's life, Time was ordered around the ritual and moral duty of prayer, at sunset, at night, at dawn and noon and the afternoon. At sunrise the men had had to leave the house, either for the fields, or to sit in the courtyard. Time was conditioned by activities such as fetching water, milking a cow, the walk to market, or the making of a blanket. Time was the changing seasons: the fire of Summer drenched by rain into the honey embers of Autumn and the dankness of Winter crept upon by the sparkle of Spring. Woven therein was Time delimited by the moon, the fast of Ramadan, the feasts of ʿid il-fitr and il ʿid il-Kabir, and the punctuation of marriage, Birth, circumcision and Death.

Presently, the regroupement centre changed all that. Numbers disordered the World, and then contrived to reorder the disorder. Wa-llahi! Activity became conditioned by Time, dependent on the springs and toothèd wheels behind the face of the clock. The segments of the day were determined by the timetable of the French military who ran KM 17. Time became divided and evaluated as Time lost and Time fulfilled; men without a job became men unemployed or underemployed. The week was conditioned by Sunday as the day of rest and worship rather than Friday. Festivals were marked by the birth and the death of the minor prophet Jesus Christ, by All Saints' Day, by Carnival and le quatorze juillet.

Azallah's home in the Kabylie village had had mud walls and a terracotta tiled roof. It had been cool in summer and warm in winter. But the house in KM 17? O what sorrow! They were allocated a dwelling with two rooms, with concrete walls and floor and a corrugated-iron roof. Verily it would be as an oven in the summer and an ice-box in the winter. The floor was no delight for bare feet. The large square windows opened their life to the outside. They were forbidden to stable their cow and not able to hollow a fire into the floor. So Azallah never again awoke in the tickle of straw, alive to mélanges of fragrance, woodsmoke and animal odour, nor guarded by the soft shadowy movements of his family rising. Ya hasra . . . in KM 17 the child awoke in a World stillborn.

Moreover, the homes in their village had had an entrance facing east, in the direction of Mecca, so when leaving the house one stepped towards the High, the Bright and the Prosperous. Now, this first morning the family had woken, stiff and cold, to the realization that the house in the regroupement centre faced west.

They had busied themselves in a conspiracy of silence. Little Moktar still lay as if life had fled him, and his grandfather took up a lump of charcoal, and blacked on to the concrete floor four times the size of what I write in the dust before me, thus:

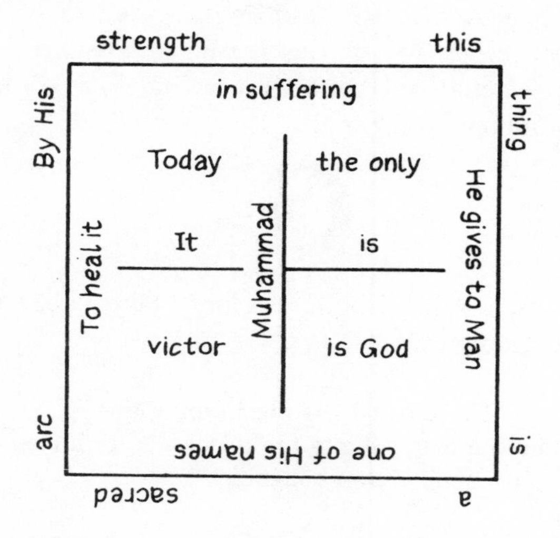

Whereupon, within this magic matrix Moktar was put, supine. Presently, as Nadia was kneeling down, arranging clothes in piles on the floor, she spoke, some splinter pricking the normal softness of her voice.

Said she, Nadia: 'Isn't it said that "all from the west brings misfortune, and can only receive darkness and sterility"?'

Upon which Azallah's grandfather turned to his son.

Said he, Hadj Ali: 'Do you want to brood inside like a hen at roost? We need to go and tend to our livestock and our prayers!'

Pay heed that the day before the family had owned sixty-three goats, thirty-four sheep, two cows and one ox, and thus were blessed by wealth. But after a hasty allocation to his son Hassan before they were parted, Hadj Ali was left with fourteen goats, twenty sheep and one cow. The five kid goats and three lambs had not survived the trek to KM 17. Now they discovered that during the night four sheep and two nanny goats had disappeared. In this clear light of the day they also beheld that the land around the centre was all planted with crops and by this reason impossible to graze. And they remembered their west-facing door – and may Allah have mercy on them all!

Sahha! So many dinars! So just before I take my leave I give you this to guess:

> These daughters live in the winds,
> and when they fall into fire they burst forth their own daughters.

And all thee who love the Prophet, may Allah bless him and grant him peace, pronounce on him the salutation!

'Blessings and greetings!'

The Third

I'm in trouble.

Yesterday my wife told me that she has an all-consuming passion for bananas. Bananas! With the first child it was grapefruit. And with the second it was pomegranates.

Could I find grapefruit? Could I find pomegranates? This country, this country! Whenever you need something, it's not to be had.

'Ya Rahwun. I know someone who can sell you bananas. (Eggs too!) Each one seven dinars ten douros.'

'Seven dinars fifty centimes! They must be enormous. A few months ago that price bought a kilo!'

Sahha! But no matter. If my wife craved onions or artichokes, wa-llah, I would lash out seventy dinars apiece because I'd be sure our third child would be a son!

On the subject of daughters, do any of you have the answer to my riddle? No one thought of pine kernels?

'Pine kernels! Tell us, ya Rahwun, what sort of child would you be expecting if your wife had a yearning for these?'

In the name of Allah, the Compassionate, the Merciful!

It is time.

Yet her name c-c-catches in my throat. It is a cadence so sweet and silvery on the tongue. Yet her name . . . catches in my throat.

I can see her in my mind. Proud and insular, and with a beauty faded, not so much by the years, or history, or the elements, but by an implacable sadness.

Many great names have known her, flirted with her, been impassioned by her, or loved her. The French novelist Gustave Flaubert spent a night with her, and noted in his journal the story of her birth.

The legend is well known (but maybe not all has been told to your wives). Some time erst a Negro and a Roman found themselves at the crossing of a river at the same time as a young girl. Now, the two men were so overcome that they all but fell in a swoon, for she surpassed in her loveliness the beauties of the world. She had a torrent of hair blacker than the night of estrangement is to an afflicted and distracted lover, her skin was marble-white and her cheeks were rosy bright, and the fullness of her breasts drew to a waist as fragile as that of a bee. Thereupon the men began to shout and rant about which of them would have her, whereupon the girl defended her honour, and told them that she would rather drown than have either touch her. The Roman then professed solicitude, and lent her his horse, and let her cross the river alone. Then the two men began to wade across together, but half-way they began squabbling anew about which of them would have the girl, and they fought in mid-stream, and the Negro was smote and killed, and his body washed back to the bank. Presently the Roman reached the other side, and hot lust stirred in him, and he pulled the maiden from the horse and overpowered her as she tried to run, thereat throwing her to the ground, and ripping off her tunic, thrust his pintle into her little slit. In the instant the girl was changed into rock, and the two men into two rivers, the Rhummel and the Bou Merzoug, condemned to flow forever around her and perpetually caress her feet.

I stress 'her'. Know it is no accident that language bestows the feminine gender on the city, and I example madinatun, stadt, ville, ciudad and cidade.

Constantine. There! Her name has finally trembled upon my lips. Constantine. Constantine.

'Qusantina in Arabic.'

Qusantina, Constantine . . . Does it matter? Or are we about to bicker over a name?

'Bône is no longer called Bône, but known, once again, as

Annaba. Philippeville is now Skikda. Boujie is now Bejaia. As you are speaking to us in Arabic—'

'—at times he speaks in French. I speak French at home with my family. I read in French. I speak Arabic, but as you can hear, not comfortably. I find it hard to read it, and with it can only write my name. There are many like me.'

'Ya sidi, Arabic is the national language now! Read our constitution!'

'And to that I reply, read our national newspaper. *El Moudjahid* is published in a French as well as an Arabic edition—'

'—for that reason I read *Ash Sha'b*.'

'And what of the Algerians who speak Tamazight? That is the mother tongue of our ancestors, yet it is being repressed whilst we are being bamboozled by Arabization and this myth of the Arab nation. Surely independence implies freedom of expression and surely—'

'Quiet, the three of you! Let our story-teller continue! Don't you know the saying, "if your friend is made of honey do not eat him up"?'

Allah ikattar hirik, ya sahib!

Now let me attempt to unravel fact from legend. Constantine was born about nine hundred years before the birth of the Prophet Muhammad (may Allah bless him and grant him salvation!). In her childhood she was indulged and spoilt by the prince Massinissa, and with her pet name Cirta, flourished as the capital of Numidia. Then later she was won by the Romans, but her childhood ended as Italy and North Africa groaned under the tyrant Maxentius, wicked guardian indeed, who tried to curb her streak of rebelliousness with the ravages of fire and the blade of the sword. And lo! she was brought from the brink of total destruction by the Emperor Constantine, and the name Constantina was took in his honour. Rome declined, she narrowly escaped ravishment by the Vandals, but not enslavement by the Byzantines, who were soon bewitched enough to bedizen her with the crude colour panoply of their civilization. Then her coming of age heralded a millennium of Islamic culture, and the tale of how this began can be thus recounted: the Arabs arrived on the outskirts, and stopped and asked their commander, Ben Djafir, how they were to conquer the city.

Said he, Ben Djafir: 'Bring me a ladder.'

That night he climbed into Constantine unseen and found all the inhabitants asleep, all except one woman.

Said he, Ben Djafir: 'Why do you not sleep?'

Said she, the woman: 'The Arabs have taken my son. I am looking for a way to find him, though I fear he is dead.'

Said he, Ben Djafir: 'Perhaps I can find him for you?'

Said she, the woman: 'You have amongst you a good man, and I am sure he will give protection to my son!'

Said he, Ben Djafir: 'What is the name of this man?'

Said she, the woman: 'Sidi Ben Djafir.'

Said he, Ben Djafir: 'That is I.'

Said she, the woman: 'In the name of Allah! Don't kill my son!'

Said he, Ben Djafir: 'Show me how to enter the town with my troops, and I will bring him with me.'

Said she, the woman: 'Come tomorrow. If my son is alive, I will open the gate for thee.'

And the next day the city fell to the Muslims.

Thereupon Constantine was the mistress of the Hafsides of Tunis for four hundred years, and then fought for and won by the Ottomans, and endued Queen of the Eastern

Beylic. She displayed her wizardry at commerce as the pre-eminent entrepôt between Tunis and the Sahara, exchanging thread of gold and silver, embroidered clothing, gilded pipes, exotic perfumes, ostrich feathers and burnouses for precious fabrics from Constantinople, rugs from Persia, silk from Syria, and Mocha coffee from the Yemen. And grain was traded with the desert for dates, wool and salt.

Algiers, our kasbah-crowned Mozghranna, fell to the French, but Constantine, stubborn madame that she was, resisted attack in the rain-and-hail-laden autumn six years on. Led by General Clauzel, the fifteen-day campaign ended with eleven officers and four hundred and forty-three men of the seven thousand troops either missing or dead. For, perched on a diamond plateau of limestone, in places swooping far down into the darksome depths of a ravine to the purl and cascade of the Rhummel, Constantine stands, almost impregnable, in dizzy disdain.

The news of the defeat of the French rapidly reached Algiers, and Constantine became extolled, and then embraced as the inamorata of us all. So, impressions of her grandeur were tattled daily there, at each and every opportunity, and ho! someone waxed prettily that seen from afar the city resembled an eagle's nest set upon a precipice.

Al-hamdu li-llah! This chatterbox happened to be seated at the time on a raffia mat next to Siddiq, as they awaited an evening's entertainment. And Siddiq recalled his vision, and gave such a gasp that his jocund neighbour leapt to his feet and hitched up his white burnous, fearing either scorpion or skulduggery. All the while Siddiq looked ahead with a lamb-like smile, and when the commotion subsided, turned and salaamed and stammered at the man.

Said he, Siddiq: '. . . you sp-sp-spoke of a giant nest atop a precipice?'

Said he, the stranger: 'Sahha! But then isn't Constantine sometimes called the City of the Air? Balak! The performance is starting!'

And lo and behold! Before them began the shadow theatre they had come to see, and soon there were cheers and laughter at the silhouette of a French soldier being set on, and mercilessly thrashed to the ground.

Thus far concerning them: but as regards Azallah Boudjemaa, his train was nearing Marseille in a deathly dawn thrust with blood-red rapiers. The compartment was sticky with the expectancies of arrival. The young soldier was twisting his cap in his hands, the priest gave a stealthy smile as he read and reread a letter scripted on rose-pink paper, and the old woman had re-formed her blue-rinse hair and was counting through a purseful of coins, causing Azallah to gnaw at an index finger and be reminded of more.

After being moved from their Kabylie village to regroupement centre KM 17, his brother Moktar remained still and silent until the day the fever began. Thereupon, Hadj Ali peeled three leaves of an onion. On the first he wrote *Thanks to God.* On the second *My God is All Powerful.* On the third *He is Good and Charitable.* Then he placed these in water and crushed them, and gave Moktar a mouthful to drink, and abluted his body with the rest. And Nadia knelt beside him and stroked his hair and softly chanted:

O Creator, O Creator,
O Thou that hast given us children!
The Creator shall come and sing you lullabies,

I shall implore God and He shall heal you,
He shall heal you and save you,
And He shall chase all evil from you.

Ya hasra. All is Allah's Decree, and there was no respite to the racing pulse, and a hacking cough came from bluish lips as searing as the sirocco, all ending in collapse and a sudden silence which his father rent by a howl to the heavens . . . *waaaaald-i!*

And the children began to wail and lament and tears coursed their cheeks, and they fell prostrate on the ground. And Nadia's heart hardened like clay.

Said Hadj Ali: 'We must remember the hadith: the Messenger of Allah, may Allah bless him and grant him peace, said that a body must be shrouded in three pure white garments, none of which is a long shirt or a turban.'

Thereupon the military doctor clattered in with an interpreter in tow. The doctor looked at Moktar, allah irahmu!, and checked his non-existent pulse.

Said he, the doctor: 'Pneumonia. It's the same old story. Malnutrition. Lack of heating. No medicine. Look, there's no furniture here, not even beds. Can't you Arabs realize it's impossible to live on a mere sou? You think that life depends on luck, this *baraka* of yours. The word in my vocabulary is idleness. Stop thinking about yourselves, but about these three children. Get yourself a job!'

Idiom and sycophancy were the ways to secure employment at KM 17. Knowledge of French could secure the good offices of army personnel. However, Mustafa knew no French, handicap indeed, for Arabic had been classified in the statute books as a foreign language twenty years before, and had yet to be voted out of its noose by the Algerian Assembly. His alternative was to seek those law-abiding internees whose linguistic skills had wheedled a meteoric rise to the élite of the colonized.

Now, the doctor had left with a snort, but the interpreter bared his dog teeth, and breathed his breath as rotten as a fart from Satan, and with his hungry hyena-eyes looked Mustafa up and down.

Said he, the interpreter, Kaddur: 'I can get you work, al-hamdu li-llah! Paid by the day. But you will need to compensate me for my trouble.'

Said he, Mustafa: 'I have no money. Leave us to our grief!'

Said he, Kaddur: 'I see you still own some livestock. As you have no money, I'll take two sheep and one goat. Then, each week, you can pay me one-half of one day's wage. Another thing: I can't get you any work looking like that. You must throw away your jellaba, burnous and turban, and wear trousers and a shirt.'

Said he, Mustafa: 'Stop the children crying! Where can I find these clothes?'

Said he, Kaddur: 'I can get them for you. And you'll need a hoe. And it's better that you pay me first.'

Said he, Mustafa: 'Sahha! But I have very little left to give you.'

Said he, Kaddur: 'I can fit you with trousers and a shirt for one more sheep and one more goat. Plus another sheep for the hoe. By the way, here I am responsible for burials, and that includes your son Moktar, may God have mercy on him! The cost will be your cow.'

Whereupon a terrible noise shook the sky, and quoth he, Hadj Ali: 'Glory be to Allah whom the thunder glorifies with His praise and the angels from the fear of Him. This is a severe warning to the people on earth.'

Wa-llah! Dressed in clothes which had lifted his children's grief with giggles, Mustafa had left each morning in an army truck to work in the vineyards of a farm some distance away. The farm was called Estepa. There he trimmed the vine shoots and hoed up weeds during the stifling spring of plots and counterplots which caused the Fourth Republic of France to fall in the minefield of the Algerian war. He picked grapes during a vintage in which the French Commonwealth went to the polls to vote in the referendum, a *oui* or a *non* for de Gaulle's remodelled constitution. And each evening he collected his wage, one hundred francs, and was ferried back to KM 17 with traces of red soil caked beneath his nails and powdering his skin.

Then with the advent of the Fifth Republic, regroupement was repackaged as rural development policy, and lo! this brought to the centre a school, open to one child per family. Suddenly KM 17 had become a bastion of privilege, ushering Azallah into the select six per cent of Muslim males literate in French, for at the Qur'anic school in his village the boy would have been a different statistic, and quite commonplace at that, as one in five of Muslim males in receipt of any primary education.

So it was that a Monsieur Durrant, his distinguished military service denoted by a short row of ribbons rainbow-edging his jacket lapel, tapped a pointer across a blackboard whilst Azallah parroted je suis, tu es, il est, nous sommes, vous êtes, ils sont, and memorized the distinction between 'vous' and 'tu', viz. tu es Arabe, *mais*, vous êtes français.

The class read about a girl named Marie and a boy named Toto. They lived in a house with curtains on large windows. They slept in beds. Their father came home from work in a suit carrying a briefcase, and read a newspaper in an armchair by the fire. Their mother made meals in a kitchen equipped with a cooker and a refrigerator, and the family all ate together, sat on chairs around a table, using a knife, fork and spoon. The family went on holidays. They travelled in a car.

The class learnt that certain weekdays were named after Mars, the Roman god of war, and Mercury, the Roman god of eloquence, skill and thieving. They learnt that their ancestors were the Gauls. They were regaled with tales of Jeanne d'Arc and accounts of the brilliance of the reign of the Sun King, Louis XIV. They were recited segments of *La Chanson de Roland*: Granz est li calz, si se levet la puldre—

'What gibberish is this?'

'Move more to the shadow. Rahwun has become intoxicated by the sun!'

Paien s'en fuient e françeis les anguissent . . . Perhaps a few coins will make me speak sense rather than Medieval French—'

'Coins or bananas?'

Li enchalz duret . . . Shukran!

Whereupon I can continue with the translation which goes something like this:

The heat is great and the dust rises;
The pagans flee and the Franks press them hard.
The chase lasts as far as Saragossa.
Bramimonde has climbed to the top of her tower,
Together with her clerks and her canons,

Whose false faith God never loved.
They have no orders and their heads are not tonsured.
When she saw the Arabs destroyed
She exclaims in a loud voice: 'Help us Muhammad!
O noble king, now our men are vanquished;
The emir is slain with such great shame.'

And not only this, but more: the children were taught that Algeria was the département of a France which stretched from Dunkirk in the north, south to Tamanrasset.

Of course, we must not forget arithmetic. Let's do some sums!

PROBLEM ONE.
On the eve of the War of Independence, the population of Algeria was approximately 9.9 million people. About one million were European settlers.
What percentage were Muslims?
Answer: 89 per cent.

That was easy! Try this. It's trickier.

PROBLEM TWO.
On the eve of the War of Independence, these one million settlers received 41.6 per cent of the national income of 548 milliard old francs. Find the average incomes per head for a) the Muslim, and b) the European, population in Algeria.
Answer: a) Muslims: 38,600 old francs.
b) Europeans: 222,980 old francs.

You enjoyed doing those averages, mes élèves? Sharpen your pencils and try one last one.

PROBLEM THREE.

630,000 Muslim agricultural holdings covered a total area of 7,349,166 hectares.
22,037 European agricultural holdings covered a total area of 2,726,700 hectares.
What were the average areas per holding?
Answer: a) Muslim farm holding: 11.6 hectares.
b) European farm holding: 123.7 hectares.

One night Mustafa came home from the farm, grape juice bloodying his hands. He had news of his brother Hassan and his family from one of the extra workers hired for the vintage. For a year they had had to live communally in a requisitioned barn with forty-three other families. Then several months later they had disappeared in the night, and no one knew where.

One night Mustafa came home from pruning the vines with the story of the European owner of Estepa from time to time putting a small box to his face and following his each and every move. And at this Nadia began to fret about the Evil Eye.

One night, then many more, Mustafa stumbled in heated with rough red wine, quaffed at the regroupement centre's café, and his side-muscles and limbs relaxed till to and fro he began to sway, and his family ran shocked away lest he do them a terrible mischief.

One night Mustafa arrived with the news that he wasn't needed again for several weeks. In twelve months he had worked precisely one hundred and seventeen days. And that was the night they noticed that his hair was fast turning white.

One night Azallah showed his father with pride what he had written that day over the arithmetic squares of his exercise book. Mustafa looked down and smiled, and then ran a finger below the clumsy characters from right to left.

Said he, Azallah: 'No, ya baba! The other way! Don't you know that!'

Said he, Hadj Ali: 'I've a moustache too.'

Little Azallah blushed at this scolding from his grandfather, blushed to the tips of his ears.

Said he, Mustafa: 'Let him bark until he is tired of it.'

Then, Azallah read, hesitantly, what he had written.

My father's car is yellow. It is big. It is fast. I love my father.

One night Mustafa writhed and moaned in pain, and Nadia summoned the interpreter Kaddur and the doctor of KM 17, noxious as they were, and bade them enter.

Said he, Kaddur: 'He says he is going to die.'

Said he, the doctor: 'Poppycock! Where does it hurt?'

Said he, Kaddur: 'He says his stomach is bursting.'

Said he, the doctor: 'Then why does he point at his kidneys? Ask him: when does it hurt?'

Said he, Kaddur: 'He says all the time.'

Said he, the doctor: 'Even in the day?'

Said he, Kaddur: 'He says especially then.'

Said he, the doctor: 'It hurts more in the day than the night?'

Said he, Kaddur: 'Now he says all the time, and it hurts more there.'

Said he, the doctor: 'There? That's his heart. Well, no need for me to recommend rest. That type always laze all day in their beds. One of those-who-do-not-like-to-work. Can spot them at a hundred metres. And my dinner was disturbed for this?'

Now, on to other matters, and the dawn when Siddiq was

leaving Algiers, the dawn that there was rain, rails of rain, so much rain that you could lap the air. It was the dawn when that thirty-eight-year-old spendthrift and zealot of the de luxe, the aristocratic Lieutenant Le Roy de Saint-Arnaud, had disembarked from the ship *Suffren* with a battalion of Legionnaires, and crossing the city quickly condemned it all as a ghastly mess. He stood horror-struck at the less than sanitary appearance of the Hôtel d'Europe, with its gross lantern overhanging the welcoming judas-set door. Whereupon Siddiq happened to pass him, and their eyes caught, and Siddiq shivered.

Shivered, as well you might too.

France: August 1973: les vacances, and the scent of bergamot wafts from the oil and cream basting the vast human rôtisserie sizzling alongside the cyan of the Mediterranean. This obsession, this vanity: the pursuit of tobacco tans.

And thereat, on August 25th (I do not have a note of the day anno Hegirae), an Algerian, thirty-seven years of age, was shot . . . dead; an Algerian, twenty-six years of age, was shot . . . dead; and an Algerian, forty years of age, was wounded . . . and later died.

In Marseille.

Now, does this racism, and let us not be polite about the word nor the deed, have at times its genesis in jealousy? For the Christians seem to covet the very colour of the skin on my hands.

Know, O my brothers, that on August 29th, an Algerian, forty years of age, was attacked and killed.

In Marseille.

Know, O my brothers, that on September 2nd, an Algerian, thirty-nine years of age, was attacked and killed.

In Marseille.

Whereupon, after inquiries into the murders, all five cases

were dropped. O Algerians! Be content to console yourselves with one of your Arab sayings: the mother of the murdered man can sleep, but the mother of the murderer cannot! Surely that is justice enough?

Ten days to Christmas. The tinsel of the festive season enlaces the Western world, and choirs croon 'peace and goodwill on earth to all men'. December 14th, and a bomb explodes at the Algerian consulate.

In Marseille.

Four dead. Twenty injured.

In Marseille.

M-a-r-s-e-i-l-l-e.

Nine letters. Nine murders in 1973 AD, AH 1393.

And here, a song, and the excuse any croak in the tenor of my voice is anger.

Hh-hem.

Allons enfants de la patrie,
Le jour de gloire est arrivé,
Contre nous de la tyrannie,
L'étendard sanglant est levé,
L'étendard sanglant . . .

And ho! my rendition of the 'Marseillaise' on the radio behind the bar of the café ended, and then zinged into a jingle, 'Euromarché, une nouvelle race de magasins . . .' And Azallah Boudjemaa's mouth was furred with sleeplessness, and a waiter brought a cup of chocolate, and a croissant which tasted meagre and dry. Azallah sat and watched a city come to life, an opportunity he rarely had. People were dunking croissants into cups or sipping their *café express*, some were reading newspapers, *Le Meridional-La France, Le Monde* or *Le Provençal*, glimpsing intermittently at their watches, and others stared into the void or the promise of the day ahead. A girl with hair as black as a moonless night, and a countenance shining and bright, and cheeks like anemones, and amorous hazel eyes, adjusted her makeup with light deft touches, and then she rose, and as she left her body swayed like a willow-branch. Then Azallah stirred his spoon in his cup to mix the dregs of chocolate while on the radio Jacques Brel warbled 'Les Bonbons'. Azallah checked his blue and white covered airline-like ticket of the *Compagnie Nationale Algérienne de Navigation*. He was sailing at midday on the SS *Tipasa* to Annaba.

Now, his uncle, aunt, his cousins, nephews and nieces were all settled in and about Algiers, and although the draw to his extended family was strong and sugared by his uncle's pledges of string-pulling him a better life there, Azallah had decided to resist it, for he needed to see his mother country with his own unenlightened eyes. So he had chosen this early winter day and selected his first destination both at random, and let Destiny blaze his road!

He paid and walked out and down the Canibière to the groves of masts and glades of sea at the old port, passed the city hall and through to the cathedral, crossing over to the Quai de la Joilette. There another ship had arrived from Tunis. Azallah watched as the douanier turned and violently jumbled the contents of the suitcases and boxes of North African arrivals, but waved the few Caucasians on with a smile.

And so it was that on the twelfth strike of midday, Azallah left that accurst city – Marseille.

And thus far concerning him, and as regards Siddiq, he was in such haste to reach Constantine and meet Lady Fate, that he too had determined to voyage by sea, and there at the jetty stood a fine ship bound from Algiers east to the port of Jijel, and Siddiq took passage on her, for despite the torrents of rain it weighed anchor that same day. But by night they had sailed into a furious squall, which tore the sails to rags and tatters so the sailors were powerless to govern the vessel as waves like mountains bore on her, and the sea was swept foaming over them. And the passengers shivered with cold, and wept for themselves, and bade one another farewell, and decried such a vile form of death. Siddiq though remained steadfast and repeated the praises of God (whose name be exalted!) and recited the Verses of Safety, namely *In God let all the faithful put their trust*, and, *Say, nothing will befall us except what God has ordained.* And lo! day broke with a happy smile and a honey sun and a favouring breeze and a blue sea barely marked by a ripple. Then there, ahoy! on the headland, Jijel stood afore them. O Allah is compassionate indeed!

Along the line of an old Roman road, and passing through valleys and glens, Siddiq travelled south two days by foot, but on the third was so overcome by loneliness that he could not restrain his tears. Then, in the early morning, he reached the deafening echoing rush of the Rhummel. Over he crossed, and overhead, bearded vultures wheeled between the stains of blackberry shadows on the sheer rock walls which soared sublime to the quiet blue of the wintertide sky. Constantine, the city which clad the summit, was unseen. The pitted road rose, and part way up, Siddiq stepped aside to make way for a groaning caravan of two hundred or more mules setting out for Tunis. Then, continuing the ascent, he overtook three donkeys straddled with clay jars a-brim with river water being coaxed up towards the city. Finally Siddiq reached the plateau, and he looked in wonderment at the landscape spread far below and dappled in greens of various hues, namely pistachio green, oil green, parrot's wing, and fine jade, and it seemed as if he were standing on the watch-tower of the world.

Then, turning, he passed between contingents of defence forces camped all about, to the city wall being topped with newly constructed battlements, and one of its gates being blocked by stones. En route he was challenged, for fear he might be a spy, but with his talk of Destiny and bird's nests, he was dismissed as a harmless fool. Whereupon he entered Constantine through al-Bab al-Jadid, therein pausing to quench his thirst from a leather cup fixed by a chain to a stone tank of water. Then he betook himself into the tangle of streets and along al-Bab al-Wadi where it seemed business as usual in the saddlers, the cobblers and the goldsmiths, the blacksmiths, the coppersmiths, the carpenters and the parchment makers which he passed in this very pattern. And presently Siddiq entered the café of Si-Likdar where voices buzzed with stories of the city's victory against the French attack just ten weeks previously. An aged man with rheumy eyes and a wheezing laugh was only too eager to recount to Siddiq the fate of a battalion of the 62nd Infantry, and I quoth: 'Ho thou! The soldiers had been on guard duty in an autumn brume so bitter that ice pellets rained from the sky, and half-froze them as the night drew in, and it was thus that they hath broken open oaken barrels of wine and eau-de-vie. They took their booty and to secrete themselves had searched out caves in the foot of the cliffs along the Rhummel. And there they fell to making merry, and were soon sozzled and befuddled and swaying to and fro, and thereupon they were jumped and all a-massacred in the mud by the brave defenders of our Constantine!'

Yet, for all these tales of bravado, there remained an atmosphere, tense and expectant, in the city.

Now, after the afternoon-prayers at the mosque of Sidi al-Kattani, as the men gathered, and grouped and conversed, Siddiq asked here and asked there if there was any who could offer him employ. Al-hamdu li-llah! Haj Muhammad Nassif, city notable, adroit merchant, and newly married to a daughter of the Bey, required someone to look after his house for, fearful of another attack by France, he was to leave with his wife and some of their family for the safety of Kairouan.

And so it was.

Meanwhile, the French had set to meditating, humiliated but not humbled, their bayonets ready sharpened for revenge. So, to quell the West, they signed and sealed a Treaty at Tafna with our national hero Abd al-Qadir, which advanced him as Sultan of the territory from Oujda, on the Moroccan frontier, across to the Oued Mijerda in Tittery and north to the sea, leaving the French free to augment their forces in the East to a formidable size, and slake their thirst for that indomitable prize, Constantine.

Tafna set alight the furnace of that summer, where trepidation ran high and the Rhummel near ran dry, and families of note and some craftsmen of repute became faint-hearted and left, but the Jews and the poorer people and the grit of the city remained.

Autumn approached, and with it came the news that France had camped south of Guelma at Medjez al-Ahma, a mere sixty kilometres as the crow flies. Whereupon, the Bey of Constantine, Al Haj Ahmed, sent proposals for peace to the French, requesting that they recognize his authority over the city and, moreover, that they promptly vacate the towns of Annaba and Guelma, part of his province.

The petition was considered little more than the scratchings of a bantam cock.

In Constantine every conversation centred around the struggle to come. Rumours bubbled that the Bey had dispatched great chestfuls of precious objects with the sweethearts of his harem up to the hill town of Mila. And endless debates focused on the best way to defend property should France succeed, and one day in the baths, the air diffused with steam and the odour of aloes-wood, as a masseur gently rubbed and pressed his sable skin, Siddiq was struck by an idea, and he took his leave, and fetched the money Haj Muhammad Nassif had left him.

Now, in Constantine as in Algiers, various groups controlled certain trades. First Siddiq approached the Kabylies who were bakers and masons. He then sought out the Negroes, whose trade was the whitewashing of walls. Next he headed off to the M'Zabites who specialized in cooked meats and vegetables, and ordered a large quantity of food. And then he returned to the Nassif house.

And lo! the following day the food arrived in several baskets. Presently a mason came and blocked up the front door with a thin wall of rubble and stones, which he faced with plaster. Then the next afternoon whitewash was splashed and brushed over the building's façade, so that, leaning out of a high window barely the size of two babouches, Siddiq spied that except for the freshness of the lime, the house in the alley seemed no more than a continuation of the adjoining properties.

'Ya Rahwun: so the proverb's true! A wall is better than a thousand good connections.'

Sahha! And may I take this opportunity to say that this is a history I cannot bear to continue.

'Not even for a few more douros?'

Know, O my brothers, that under the command of Damrémont, twelve thousand three hundred troops marched upon Constantine, blazing the countryside with the fabulousness of their uniforms as if to woo, and not wage war, on this tigress of Algeria. But even the red vest and fez of the Chasseurs d'Afrique, the short blue jacket, oriental trousers and green turban worn by the Zouaves, and the various flowing red burnouses, and the dazzle of gold braid, were insufficient to combat the gloom of another premature onset of winter, more ice-rain, and more sodden ground.

On October 5th (I cite the date anno Domini once again for reasons you will shortly see) the army arrived, and bivouacked at Sidi Mabrouk, across the Rhummel gorge, eye to eye with Constantine.

On the 6th they were bombarded by gunfire and insulted by the shrill yells and *youyouyous* of women from the roofs of the city.

The following day a morale-destroying three thousand Arab horsemen appeared from nowhere, and seemeth a big white and grey shroud flying through the air as they charged two squadrons camped but four hundred paces from the city gates and then, at the first defensive fire, just turned and took themselves away.

On the night of the 7th, the army camped across the

Rhummel were surprised, and jumped and attacked by guerrillas.

On the 8th the troops were plagued by yet more ice-rain.

On the 9th the battery opened fire on the west of the city, the cannons booming until the evening, to strike terror into the defenders' souls. Whereupon a Turk was assigned to present a proclamation to the people and their Bey:

CITIZENS OF CONSTANTINE!

My cannons are at the foot of your walls; they are going to be tilted, and my troops will enter in your city. If you wish to prevent great misfortune, surrender whilst there is still time. I guarantee you by oath that your women, your children, and your possessions will be respected, and that you will continue to live peacefully in your homes.

Send good people to speak to me and agree everything, before I enter in the town; I shall give them my seal, and that I have promised,

Comte de Damrémont.

No need for a postscript: remember Algiers?

The reply, written on behalf of the city by Ben Aissa, read something like this:

If you lack gunpowder we will send you it; if you have no biscuits, we will share ours with you; but you will never enter this city. France will only be master of Constantine when we have all been killed.

Now, the audacity of this missive left the enemy speechless and thirsting for blood. The army manoeuvred into position to bombard the minx taunting them from across the yawning ravine. Then, the morning of the 12th, Damrémont was killed in an attack, and command passed to the morose sexagenarian General Valée, and the fighting was spurred by a vengeance, for the honour of France, the African Empire, and perhaps the world was at stake!

And then! A message arrived from the Bey, requesting a ceasefire for four and twenty hours and a peace conference set under way.

The French reply was curt, agreeing if the gates of the city were opened there and now.

October: Friday 13th, a day, a date, deemed jinxed. Yet the dawn broke into an azure sky which roused the hearts of the soldiers as they massed before the city wall. There was a silence, and then the cry: *Enfoncé Muhammad! Jésus-Christ prend la semaine!*

'Ya Rahwun . . .'

Oh! In Arabic: Muhammad is done for! Jesus Christ is duty officer this week!

'Sahha!'

As if thunder overhead, gun and cannon fire exploded endlessly. Yataghans swung and cut, bayonets thrust and stabbed. By nine, the two enormous crimson standards which had floated over the city gates had been lowered and the tricolour hoisted amidst cries of 'Vive le Roi!' Then once through the first wall, the troops charged through gunfire from loyal citizens picking off the enemy from their houses, and breached the second inner wall.

Already men, women and children were trying to flee, shinning down hemp ropes into the canyon, down ropes which snapped beneath the weight of too many souls, crashing human chains into the chasm to the Rhummel. Soldiers ranged through the city in search of food, changing their soiled and vermin-ridden uniforms for burnouses and tunics as they went, some of which were new, some freshly laundered, and some stripped from the bodies of the dead. The streets were choked with smoke and dust, and heady with the stench of butchery and death. Mutilated and disfigured corpses lay knee high in the lanes and narrow alleys. Turned frenzied and frantic by the red flood of blood, by the carnage and the fever of rape, the pillage tore on through cries of victory, glory, and total despair. Two hours this lasted, some say; others tell of a sickness of three long days.

Le Roy de Saint-Arnaud, now a captain in the Legion, stroked his goatee beard and twirled his handlebar moustache as he later wrote: *In Constantine, if I had wanted, I could have been a thief . . . I would have been able to take from a chest sufficient to pay my debts and be tranquil. But I was drunk with gunpowder and glory. I wanted nothing to sully this . . .*

And were it be that there had been more like him! For souvenirs of Constantine soon became the rage of the Christian settlers, riff-raff and rich alike, and browsing in the Place Rovigo in Bône they would purchase the weapons, carpets, dresses and jewels thieved from our heroic city. Eight hundred stolen Arabic tomes, there including a history of Cirta through the centuries, a geography of the East Indies, and an account of the Empire of Sarrazins by Makay of Tlemcen, had been saved from the fire and prised with silver from the infantries' mitts, al-hamdu li-llah! rescued, but destined for the private world of France's bibliothèque in distant Algiers.

But I lose my thread. On October 14th 1837 AD, a proclamation was posted, and read thus:

SOLDIERS!

The tricolour flies over the walls of Constantine. Honour is paid to your persistence and bravery. The enemy's defence has been hard and stubborn; your attacks have been more dogged still. The artillery, by unbelievable efforts, were able to breach and destroy the wall, an assault managed with much intelligence and executed with great valour, finally rendering us masters of the place. By this success you have avenged the death of your brave comrades fallen at your sides, and gloriously compensated for the defeat of last year. You deserve well of your country and King, they will know to compensate your efforts.

Now spare the city, respect the property and the inhabitants and handle carefully the resources that it holds for the future needs of the army.

The lieutenant-general, commander-in-chief of the Constantine expedition,

Comte Valée

Of the French Army, one hundred soldiers were killed, forty-eight expired of illness, and five hundred and six were wounded. Recorded, moreover, was that two hundred and thirty-seven horses died in total.

And the number of dead and wounded of the courageous citizens of Constantine?

The numbers seem not to exist – or dare not be remembered.

Symbol of what was to come, that day, outside the city wall, two communal graves were dug for the dead.

One for the French. And one for we Algerians.

Wa-llah. It is as the poet did express himself in these verses:

> My heart is devoured by an ardent flame
> Because the Christians have taken Constantine.
> The spirit of my heart like my soul is saddened,
> I cry, I wail, my sobs oppress me,
> They have seized the gardens and the city,
> Yet, the gunpowder explodes, our guns are cocked and loaded.
> O ardour of my heart, let the flow of my tears!
> Algiers has fallen to their swords, Annaba is between their hands,
> Nothing remains, their weapons are master . . .
> Yet, the gunpowder explodes, and our guns are cocked and loaded.

This, then, is that which has reached us of History, and glory be to Him who endureth for ever and for aye, and by whose will interchange the Night and the Day.

'You cannot close there!'

'What of Siddiq?'

'Bi-llahi: tell us that at least.'

Next week – if the rewards of today are incentive enough for me to return . . . Wah! What has prompted such munificence? Shukran!

'Ya Rahwun! Aren't you going to pose us a riddle?'

Inshallah! Hmm: I give you this to guess:

A bird, born in the morning, lives one day,
The night comes, he gathers his feathers and he flies away.

The Fourth

As you know, the worth of a sheep is judged by the fat in its tail. Now, a friend of mine took his son to the souk here one day to demonstrate this principle. Whereupon, a few days later, his son came running to meet him as he returned from the mosque.

Said he, the son: 'Ya baba! I came home from school to find a strange man here in our house! I think he wants to buy my mother.'

'We have the answer to your riddle: it is the sun!'
No my friends: it is the souk, that is the word.

In the name of Allah, the Compassionate, the Merciful!
Now watch, O my brothers, as I take up this handful of

sand and then let it trickle through my outstretched fingers. The grains are like people, like events, like memories. They may brush each other once, or never at all. Then, however much I scuff at them, or stir them, however indulgently the wind blows them, those which had chanced to touch one another before may, or may never, do so again.

And so it was, that as the passengers boarded the SS *Tipasa* at that diabolical city, Marseille, in front of Azallah Boudjemaa stood Michel, or Mike as he was known in the United States, Ardales.

It is said that his great-grandfather, a Spanish peasant, Juan Pedro Ardales, robbed a fortune from a grandee then slew him with a stone, in a bodega vaulted by sunbeams, one siesta, one broiling summer in Andalucia. He had fled, sleeping by day, travelling by the milk white of moonlight, along the coast to Malaga, where he took a passage on the first ship to set sail, chanced to be bound for Algeria.

On board, in third class, he took heed of the hubbub of the emigrants which competed with the noise of the engines and the sound of the sea, and which spoke in the following manner: '. . . sí Señores, Algeria is the El Dorado of Africa . . . no, there is no reason to worry about the land and the natives . . . por qué? The French have split tribally owned land into privately owned pieces nicely undermining tribal cohesion and the rule of the chiefs . . .' 'Señor! Don't forget the Warnier Act last year which let property be sold to Europeans, and opened vast tracts of fertile land for sale along the coastal plains . . .' 'Sí, and I heard that it all but forced the Muslims to sell up for next to nothing, and they had little option but to work as labourers for a pittance. Now I must attend to my son, he's been seasick again. My brother'll tell you of the Jewish lawyer's clerk near Mostaganem. Perdóneme . . .' 'Well, this clerk, he bought two hundred and ninety-two hectares of land, tenanted by five hundred and twelve no, five hundred and thirteen Muslims, for a mere twenty francs! No wait, Señores, let me finish . . . the best is yet to come. This clerk, he cunningly imposed costs on the "vendors" totalling eleven thousand francs, which forced them to work for him to pay the debt off . . .' 'Our main worry is health: someone told me yesterday about a village, Clauzel-Bourg I think he said, settled by German families, and after only forty days four fifths of them were bedridden, and many were dead before the village was evacuated. Of what? Malaria. Typhoid. Cholera. Todo . . .' 'Sí, another settler's village, Zurich, was decimated by cholera . . .' 'Boil your water, Señorita!' 'Most of the land is no more than mosquito-infested swamp, but with good drainage . . .' 'Cereal makes money, certainly, but Señores, viniculture can make eight times more profit per hectare: in fact, you need only to employ Muslims for fifty or sixty days a year to prune and harvest if you're very careful. Thanks be to God: someone's sighted land . . . Buena suerte!'

So the steamer docked at Oran, but having learnt of the city's large Spanish community, Ardales thought it wiser to make his way eastwards. He rode overland by horse, and there is a story, handed down to his children and children's children like an emerald the size of a hazelnut, of how, stopping at Boufarik, south-west of Algiers, he asked for 'une consommation', and was served neither anisette nor cognac, but a capsule of quinine.

'Ya Rahwun, I heard that everyone whose face became sallow

with fever in the early years of colonialism was said to have had the "Boufarik complexion"!'

Sahha, ya-sitt!

And it was on the eastern edge of the Mitidja that Ardales bought a thirty-seven-hectare property. It was, originally, a scrap of the tracts of land sequestered by France as war indemnity for the two thousand three hundred and eighty-six French lives lost during the unsuccessful revolt led by our hero Muhammad Mukrani, territory thereupon sold for a trifle, in this case to a refugee from Alsace and Lorraine after the forfeit of that province to a triumphal Prussia. However, the ex-factory worker had not dug into agricultural life, for his heart a-yearned for a city.

The new owner Ardales named the farm Estepa, in memory of the village in which he was born. Following the only occupation that he knew, he began cultivating vines, and soon the red grapes on the red soil exorcized the ghosts of the white grapes on the chalk of Jerez. He also invested capital in pressing cellars and vats, and hired them at the vintage to smaller or less foresighted farmers in the locality than he.

Then by his fortieth birthday, some bouncing baby had burst forth and landed plonk! tipping the demographic scales and lo! the number of Europeans born in Algeria outweighed the total number of immigrants; and the infant's wails were the trumpet flourish of the appearance of a new people, come to be called the *pieds-noirs*. The origins of the name? Perhaps from the view of metropolitan Frenchmen that the settlers' feet were burned black by too much African sun—

'—or because they wore black shoes rather than babouches.'

'Sahha! Or because the naval ratings from the engine-room had at one time stepped ashore with their bare feet black from coal-dust. The reasons are numerous.'

Now, shortly afterwards the dashing and greying Juan Pedro Ardales had plighted his troth and wed the fizgig youngest daughter of a local Italian, whose family had fled the unification and gained respectability as traders in Rouiba. It was just two years before the close of the nineteenth Christian century when Ardales and his bird-witted bride had arrived in Algiers en route to a honeymoon in the French Riviera, and from the room of their hotel they were spectators to riots and looting by a mob of five thousand pieds-noirs, whereupon, putting aside their opera glasses, the couple fell to clasping and embracing and cooing and biting and mad intertwining of legs, and then he mounted and they began a-bucking to and fro, with a motion so pleasant now fast and now slow to the beat of yells of 'A bas les juifs!', 'Vive l'armée!' and 'A bas Zola!' till at last he sank down on the blood-spotted sheet and she swooned away. And the following day, as they clip-clopped in the creaking fiacre off to the quays, they passed shops and cafés, some partly, some totally destroyed, and the unblemished all armoured with paper signs reading *Magasin*

Français, Magasin Catholique and *Ce magasin n'est pas juif.* And Juan Pedro spoke the language of love, a discourse of how usury was the scourge of Algeria, and how the Jew had surely misused all the power he had in handling money, so deserving this wrath upon him, and a dutiful Madame Ardales agreed.

They endured four children, one boy and three girls, and also survived the plague of phylloxera bugs which ruined three in ten of their neighbours in the years before the Great War, whereby Estepa expanded to seventy-three hectares. And Juan Pedro died in the very year that Boumédienne was born predestined to lay the foundations of our present nation.

Now, Ardales' son and grandson, the begetter of Michel, focused on the production of a quality wine, and two years before our War of Independence began, the Domaine d'Estepa was rated as a *Vin Delimité de Qualité Supérieure*, and poured into a polished glass it was as deep and black as a Sahara night with a purple intensity at the rim, and its bouquet was clean but complex, and its palate was heady, tannic and acid but refreshingly so, with a savoury flavour which lingered long . . .

. . . but not, al-hamdu li-llah!, long enough, for the War began, and like many they stopped replacing the old vines with new. Michel's grandfather died the month that the Fourth Republic fell. And although the visit of de Gaulle the following month drove the pieds-noirs to a frenzy as he stretched a V-sign wide above his head and proclaimed 'Je vous ai compris', the reaction of Juan Pedro Ardales' petit-fils was to buy a cine camera and catalogue the life of Estepa. So with his Kodak Zoom 8 he took film of the fellahin, some arriving from the nearby regroupement centre KM 17, and who variously pruned the vines and harvested the vintage, or led the horse carts collecting the baskets of grapes to take to the fermenting vats, and who worked in the bottling plant and the cuvier: so it was that Mustafa Boudjemaa gained unwitting immortality!

And Ardales filmed the arcades, verandas and Moorish windows of their two-storey house, and shot film of their servants, robed in white, topped with a red fez and wearing white gloves, attendant in rooms of elegant furniture, fine china and wrought silver, and glittering crystal chandeliers. And he filmed the traditional Easter Monday family picnic pivoted around the breaking of the sweet hemispherical cake, the mouna. And reels and reels of more.

Then, with the ceasefire in the eighth year of the war, an Algerian approached Ardales, offering to buy Estepa for what amounted to the annual profit of just five hectares of vines. Ardales refused, and at that moment decided to stay on after Independence, and weather the storm if any, and at least start replacing vines which would be too old for production three years hence. Forty-eight hours later, a family on the neighbouring property were found with their throats cut, and the men with their sexual organs stuffed in their mouths. Within hours, Ardales had dismissed the servants and dispatched his wife and children, Pierre, Isabel and Michel, with an army escort to Algiers to embark for France. Thereupon he went and knelt at the marble headstone which marked the graves of the previous two generations of his family on Estepa, and pleaded forgiveness for that which he was about to do, and his tears ran down his cheeks like a copious rain, and he wept violently until he fell prostrate and all but fainted. Then that night he drove away, drove as the backdrop of fulgent flames torched the diaphanous blackness of the sky, and gobbled the farm machinery, the cuvier and the chais with its vats and barrels and cases of wine, and horses screamed, and fires raged all night and merged with the green-tinged cinnabar dawn, having devoured the wood, and blitzed the china, glass and crystal which had gleamed and sparkled wealth and welcome in their home. He had taken nothing with him but a small leather case crammed with cans of cine film.

The family had gone to Paris, but fled the greyness, for the sun of California. There Ardales bought a dilapidated winery in the Napa Valley, and was soon reliant upon Mexican grape-pickers, gardeners, and domestics. Yet despite the adopted country, the success of a new wine, the three Mercedes automobiles, the proud white house, the glinting blue of the swimming-pool, and the hiss of apple-green lawns watered by spinning jets, Ardales and his wife still feared the soughing of one word, Algérie. Ever more often they sat in silence to the whirr and flicker of re-runs of already re-run cine-films of Estepa . . . *look: there's Mustafa trimming vines; look: there's Mustafa treading grapes, what a goofy smile!* . . . and they knew how it felt not to be free.

Their son Michel had no interest in wine other than for consumption, having discovered an academic talent and a latent interest in the Orient. He was awarded a Fulbright Islamic Civilization grant to study the history of city development in Algeria.

And so it was that Azallah Boudjemaa and Michel Ardales both stepped one before the other on to the SS *Tipasa*.

Wa-llahi! What I'm saying is this. A stranger is the relative of every other stranger.

Spilling through my hand, these grains of sand are the bedrock of Algeria.

And embarking on that noble ship, *Tipasa*, Michel Ardales

took passage in first class, and Azallah Boudjemaa in economy down below, and they weighed anchor and set sail on the blessing of Allah Almighty and on His aidance and His favour to bring the voyage to a safe issue. And Azallah stood on a narrow fringe-deck braced against the chill air and watched the city I spoke of as wretched happily diminish as they passed to sea beyond the infamous Château d'If.

It was a twenty-four-hour crossing, and the afternoon gathered into a passage of greyness, the sea churning and the sky scudding alloys of silver, uranium, iron and lead. Inside Azallah sat at random in one of the empty green vinyl seats, and drugged by the drone of the engines, the mugginess of the cabin and the light rolling of the ship, his eyes fell closed and his mind swam on through the ebbs and flows of recollection.

And lo! at KM 17 they had received the news that Azallah's uncle and his family were living in Algiers at somewhere called Nador-Scala, and with these tidings Mustafa's mysterious ailments were cured. And slyly he sold the last of their sheep and their goats, and obtained permission for his family for a day in Rouiba, ostensibly to buy provisions. Then once there they all hurried on to the first bus set to depart for Algiers.

Azallah had sat next to Hadj Ali, his face pressed against the window as they drove into the city, stunned by excitement as they passed so many buildings such as he had never before seen, as they passed countless vehicles: military tanks, motorcycles, scooters, cars, lorries and trolley-buses. The crowded pavements pulsed less with the people than the ever-shifting mottle of their clothing. The flowing white haik of Arab women; the white coiled turban of the Arab men; the long-visored lizard cap, the berets or helmets, and plain green or camouflage green-beige-and-cream of France's militia; pied-noir women dressed in all colours of jumpers, skirts and blouses, and the odd pillbox hat; and pied-noir men in dark suits, white shirts and sharp coloured ties, or red checked shirts and drain-pipe denims. And between the buildings were fleeting vistas of an endlessness of sorcery, the peacock-blue sea.

Now, Nador-Scala was a bidonville sited in the south of Algiers not far from the markets, docks and abattoirs. From a question on direction, it transpired that two zones of Nador-Scala were settled by the tribal groups of the Oulad Amara and the Oumelakhoua from the Saharan Atlas, the Ouannougha from the Tell Atlas, and the Bitham from H'dna. They were pointed to a third area, for the most part settled by people from the Kabylie. They picked their way through the snaking alleyways doubling as gutters, between the shacks stood cheek by jowl in a haphazard jumble of corrugated iron, sheet metal, mud and reeds, with never an outside window. They squeezed by a donkey with a basket of garbage slung from its back, and then ahead Azallah spied his uncle, Hassan, and cousin Rashid.

And they wept and rejoiced with joy exceeding, and they talked, talked of the present and not the past, whereupon an awkwardness lashed like a whip between them. Then they talked of work.

Most of the tribal groups were employed in a particular type of employ: the Bitham worked in the abattoirs, the Oulad Amara as stevedores in the markets. Hassan worked in the fish market, and offered the chance for Mustafa to assist him, and would pay his wages from his own pocket. Thereupon he fared on with the news that his elder son Sa'id found occasional employ as a longshoreman; ten-year-old Rashid went from café to café selling combs and shoe laces, and as a final shock, his wife, Latifa, worked as a maid in a pied-noir flat in nearby Diar al-Mahsul.

Hadj Ali and Mustafa said nothing.

Said he, Hassan: 'To get anywhere we must find better jobs. But it all depends on string-pulling – "le piston". The system is corrupt. When the war against France is won, inshallah, when we have a free Algeria, there will be no more pull. There will be equal opportunities for all. And that is the way it should be.'

So it was that Nadia cooked and cleaned for the two families, and Mustafa rose daily in darkness, and went with his brother to the fish market, and returned tainted with the scent of the sea, and every so often silver scales would glint upon his hands.

And Azallah joined his cousin and became a vendor of gum and pencils and sometimes biro-pens, out in the centre of the city where the buildings rose white as a very white pigeon all around. Didn't Nadia often say that white days were happy days? The boys would leave Nador-Scala and cling to the rail outside a trolley-bus as far as al-Bab al-Wadi. From the rusting equestrian statue of the Duc d'Orléans in the Place du Gouvernement they would wander along the vendors selling sweetcakes, merguez and, to the call of 'Fraîche, fraîche', lemonade, occasionally in receipt of some morsel, gratis. They would pass soldiers with sub-machine-guns to wend their way through the mountainous labyrinth of the kasbah. Later, back on the boulevards, they would peep in at the mass of items on sale in the Galeries de France, or glimpse into the exotic palm courtyard of the Hôtel Aletti. Then up along the Rue Michelet where young men and women sat at tin tables, sipping Martini and Campari and soda, bickering over the literature of Voltaire, Simone de Beauvoir or Genet, or swooning over such cinematic stars as Jean-Paul Belmondo, Alain Delon and Brigitte Bardot. So they walked, hour after hour, day after day, and although the concrete pavements and tar macadam and cobble streets were hard on Azallah's naked feet, he was too absorbed in the city about him to either flag or cripple. And even the rain intoxicated the senses, the torrents of water which drummed on the metal roof of their shack and flooded the floor, which cascaded in cataracts before the arcades along the Boulevard Carnot, and which blurred and threatened the entire city with liquescence.

However, Azallah was not alone in his sensibility to Algiers. Hadj Ali had drawn into himself since their arrival, and his body had become hunger-lean and his eyes lacklustre as if his spirit had died. Once he had been respected as the elder of their village, and the owner of a hundred-plus livestock. But O woe and alack! for his opinion was not now asked, not even by his sons, who begged instead for the deliberations of some stranger less than half their father's age. Now this stranger had an ill-omened phiz, he owned no cows, nor sheep nor goats, and he had yet to make the pilgrimage to Mecca. Yet he was omniscient because he spoke French correctly, because he dressed like a European in a suit and a tie, because he had a stable lucrative job with paid holidays, and because his children received education and read Tin-Tin and magazines. Cos he moved like a rat through the bureaucratic nightmare of pied-noir Algeria.

And wa-llahi! Azallah would oft gaze with his grandfather out to the sea, and if not distracted by the laughing and splashing of young pieds-noirs as they indulged in a swim, Hadj Ali would instruct his grandson on that precious quality Honour, and tutor him in the tenets of Islam, and thereupon he would always speak in handsome terms of the great-great-great uncle of Azallah, the revered marabout, Si Abd Allah.

And at other times he would wax merry, and relate some delightsome story of mysterious meaning, and the most important of these, concerning the coffee and the milk, I quoth:

There was once in times of yore and in ages and times long gone before a good and kind King, who deeply loved his subjects, and so determined was he to rid his Kingdom of all iniquity that he crossed mountains and valleys galore, so that he himself could personally administer justice.

Now this monarch was a simple and a modest man. His travels were made with neither pomp nor trump, with a small entourage of bodyguards, a chef and the person in charge of his coffee, his qahwadji.

And the King would sit in the shade at the foot of a tree, and there listen to the complaints of his people. Thereupon his qahwadji would gather some twigs and a variety of dry plants, and then prepare between two stones a fire on which he set his little kettle, filled with the sweetest water and the finest of Yemen coffee which released as it stewed a stimulating and delirious aroma. He also bought from poor people the milk of their goat or their ewe, and this he heated separately.

Then, from the corner of his improvised hearth, the qahwadji would watch the succession of complainants, and whenever there was a lull, he would hurry to the King with his tray and deliver a little song:

Here is the coffee, the coffee and the milk,
You entirely salute the beloved Prophet,
And he who digs a pit against his brother,
Will be the first to be swallowed there.

No one could understand the quatrain, but no matter! The King was revived by this coffee during his long audiences, but he always took strict care to mix into it the milk to sweeten the beverage and whiten its colour.

Now, the qahwadji had served the King for thirty years, and his jellaba was always impeccably clean and stretched to his finger tips, and his hamma was of the finest fresh muslin wound around his head and the lower half of his face revealing only his eyes.

One day, some ne'er-do-well, jealous of the qahwadji and the confidence with which he was held by the King, determined to take his place. Waiting for a moment when the King was alone, this pup approached him.

Said he, the knave: 'Sire, forgive me. But I cannot hold back what I have come to know.'

Said he, the King: 'And what, pray, is this?'

Said he, the rapscallion: 'Dost thou know why thy qahwadji forever has the bottom of his face veiled?'

Said he, the King: 'It is his custom.'

Said he, the rat: 'The man is rotten to the core and his breath is so fetid that were it not for the veil, thy coffee would be infected with this horrible odour.'

The King was astounded. Was this the reason that his qahwadji was so modest, that he slept apart and lived beyond the city walls, and at the call for the dawn prayer was the first at the city gates to be admitted to the palace?

The King left and called his servants, and commanded that on the morrow they must wait at the gates and seize the first man to arrive, and take him, and hang him.

Now, this lowest of the low thought it wise to be at the palace the following dawn to request the job of qahwadji. However, in so doing he arrived afore him, whereupon he was taken and hanged.

When, later that day, the King saw the qahwadji in his customary white clothes, he fell about stupefied. And bearing his coffee the qahwadji sang:

> Here is the coffee, the coffee and the milk,

and the King listened carefully to the rest:

> You entirely salute the beloved Prophet,
> And he who digs a pit against his brother,
> Will be the first to be swallowed there.

Thereupon the King summoned his guards, and checked that they had executed the first at the gates that morning. And hearing their response, he asked the qahwadji why his face was aye covered.

Said he, the qahwadji: 'Sire, when I search for twigs I may happen to bruise herbs, releasing certain noxious odours; and when the fire is lit, the cinders or the blackness of the smoke could soil my body and my face.

'Does it not suit you that your servant is as white as the milk that he serves you, as the prayer of the Prophet, may Allah bless him and grant him peace, and as the justice which God gives you?'

'Ya Rahwun! You are playing with us. These stories aren't stories but riddles. What do they really mean?'

And I reply to you with this riddle of riddles from Abd as-Samed:

Ala. It is a great falsehood. The earthenware jar has been broken, and the oil remains in abeyance.

'The oil is ice?'

'So it seems, judging from our story-teller's sudden frozen expression.'

'Perhaps a dinar or two will melt the answer from his throat?'

Shukran! The word of the riddle is – a riddle!

Now, on occasion, Azallah and his cousin Rashid would wait outside shops or the central market, and should they see a European woman laden with groceries and parcels, would run up beside her with the cry, 'Portez, Madame?'

One day they had just earned a few coins thus, and were returning to Nador-Scala through Diar al-Mahsul, when from a third-floor balcony a voice called to them.

Said she, Rashid's mother: 'Ya Rashid!'

They looked up, but her smile faded as she was joined by a blonde with bare shoulders.

'Boys, come up!' she cried with a wave.

Rashid's mother nodded nervously. Azallah and his cousin walked into the entrance and up stairs which smelt faintly of disinfectant. The lady with the blond hair was waiting at an open door. Rashid's mother stood behind, looking uncomfortable. Instinctively the boys avoided looking at the face of the woman.

'Come in, come in.'

They entered the flat. The walls were flower-white, and the furniture cushions, primary red, blue, and yellow-bright.

Metal lamps with conical shades were poised on low wooden tables, or free-standing and angled at a piece of a Tuareg blanket framed on the wall. Large windows opened on a partial view of the bay. Through a door a pubescent girl with brown plaits paced into the room. Azallah and Rashid saw the scowl on her face before lowering their eyes to the terracotta tiles beneath their feet.

'Maman, what are these dirty Arab boys doing here?'

'This is Fatima's son,' she said, pointing a finger at Azallah. 'And this is her nephew,' she added, pointing to Rashid. 'Say hello!'

'No!'

Their hostess ran her hand through her hair, exposing dark roots, and gave a wan smile.

'How old are you?' she asked.

'Ten,' replied Rashid.

'I have seven years,' replied Azallah.

'You don't look seven and ten,' said the girl. 'You both look a lot older. My father says all Arabs are liars, and it looks like he's right. You're born like that.'

'Skout!' snapped maman.

The five stood as if an asp was gliding between them around the floor. The girl started to softly tap the surface of the sideboard with her knuckles: dit-dit-dit dah-dah . . .

'Stop that!'

'I won't. This is our country. Algérie française. Algérie française, jusqu'à la mort! That's what papa says. We'll never leave. Never, never, never . . .' And she ran from the room with a sob.

A troop of ants were marching along the skirting. Presently the woman sighed, and turned to Latifa.

'Fatima, how about giving the boys some of the delicious

cinnamon sherbet you made this morning, if it's cooled.' She clapped her hands, and added, 'Allez! Fissa! Fissa!'

She led Azallah and Rashid out on to a small terrace. A tub of bougainvillaea swelled trails of red starlets, some pendulating in the breeze. And on a green table, half-covered by a white linen cloth, lay a crescent of crimson watermelon.

Whereupon the sea pounded, the air sprayed and gusted, and clouds, massed and charred, spurted, revealing a fragment of starriness here, and a glimpse of a silver half-moon there.

The sea was moving, the sky was moving, the ship was moving: Azallah was dizzy with the feeling that he was the victim of Time, and his hands gripped the wooden rail of the *Tipasa* tighter, willing everything to stop, as if the instant would give him a moment to grab control.

Night, and around him the water pounded like the thud of la strounga, the plastic explosives which punctured the curfew in Algiers. And every so often, from the bidonville at Nador-Scala, they would hear a far-off klaxon sound out, dit-dit-dit dah-dah.

Al-gér-ie fran-çaise.

That summer, the last year of the war, the Organisation Armée Secrète, the infamous OAS composed of civilians and military deserters and specializing in terrorism, scored their first propaganda success as they took over the television and broadcast a recorded message for Muslims and Europeans to join them and to fight against the dictatorship of de Gaulle. And in the streets the pieds-noirs used their car horns to hammer out their response: *dit-dit-dit dah-dah, dit-dit-dit dah-dah ...*

About a month later there was a second pirate transmission: for five hours it threw the pieds-noirs into a frenzy and they thumped their car horns once again or clanged their anthem on saucepans from their windows and their balconies: *dit-dit-dit dah-dah, dit-dit-dit dah-dah, dit-dit-dit dah-dah . . .*

Explosions thudded throughout the city. Check points were set up for control. Trolley-buses were grilled against attack, and the black and white of OAS banners and balloons hung or floated from their overhead cables. And the whiteness of the walls of Mozghranna were soiled by the terror of:

OAS
VAINCRA!

Three days after the Christians fêted their New Year, unknowingly for the last time in Algeria, red, white, and blue edged posters slapped across the city walls ordered all European and Muslim males of military age into the ranks of the OAS.

Dit-dit-dit dah-dah, dit-dit-dit dah-dah, dit-dit-dit dah-dah . . .

OAS
VAINCRA!

BANG!

Blown-up front-page newspaper photographs of four-and-a-half-year-old Delphine Renard and the wrecked playroom at 19 bis Avenue Victor Hugo, Paris. The OAS's intended victim, the Minister of Culture, André Malraux, had been absent that day. Instead a child loses her right eye and suffers a hundred stitches in a glass-gashed face.

At last, after seven years of war, a Paris newspaper screamed: France wants no more of this!

Paris; and the following day, ten thousand people demonstrate, chanting 'O-A-S As-sas-sins!' and the potent cocktail of one nervous police force, one hostile crowd and three hours of skirmishes fizzed until the police went berserk and charged at the intersection of the Boulevard Victor Hugo and the Rue Charonne. Whereupon eight were dead and one hundred demonstrators and one hundred and forty police injured.

Wa-llahi! Seven years of war, but it was this two-day tally in France's capital city which contrived the ceasefire at the beginning of spring, and hastened negotiations for peace at Evian.

And Azallah's family chattered excitedly of returning to their village in the Kabylie, of rebuilding their home and their former lives. Thus the weeks passed a-flight, till one disreputable dawn, of pastel shade and resplendent light, Azallah's cousin Saʿid, a sturdy, stout, broad-shouldered wight, headed for the hiring hall, near the Quai de Calvi, to wait for work with fellow dockers. The time was 6:10.

BANG!

A truckload of scrap metal exploded. Whereupon sixty-two were dead, and one hundred and fifty injured.

And in the antiseptic air of the hospital, Saʿid lay a hero, grinning to the tearful visitors from the whiteness of his iron bed. None of them had seen his other face, the look when the doctor had a-thrown back the sheet, and Saʿid had known that he had no limbs below his thighs.

Night had fallen as Azallah and Hadj Ali returned one evening from the hospital. They took a short cut, wary of being caught in the curfew, and then froze at a cry and a scuffle, and a window light silhouetted a French serviceman with an arm drawn across his throat before being beaten by two men as he slumped in the alley. Unbeknown to them, on this day after il ʿid il-Kabir, attacks by the OAS and the FLN murdered someone in the streets of Algiers on average every fifteen minutes.

Presently, seeing the struggle all but lost, the OAS ranged through the city, and burned down the University Library and the new Préfecture. Thereupon, in a rush one morning, Azallah and his father and grandfather and mother and sisters were rallied to help Hassan move his family into the flat where his wife had worked in Diar al-Mahsul, for it had been abandoned. In the street outside the charred remains of furniture glowed and mattresses smoked. And reaching the flat, they saw in it naught, but found it as the poet said:

> The chambers were like a beehive well stocked;
> when their bees quitted them they were empty.

For inside, the rooms had been reduced to boxy voids, save for a thousand fragments of china and glass strewn over the floors like a petrified fall of leaves and blooms. And in the refrigerator, on a white enamelled plate, lay a sausage of shit.

Azallah's aunt was chopfallen and wept and ran amok, whereupon Hassan showed her a plate, patterned with gentle flowers, which he had salvaged from the debris on the floor. She calmed herself and smiled and handed it to Nadia.

Said she, Azallah's aunt: 'I'm going to be happy here, here in my new home.'

And Nadia let the plate drop and to the floor it crashed, and smashed.

And so, O my brothers, after eight years of war, in a

collective admission of culpability, eight hundred and fifty thousand Europeans fled in a matter of weeks clutching their two-suitcase entitlement, leaving flats, leaving houses, leaving tables, chairs, sofas, radios, gramophones, records and televisions, leaving cookers and refrigerators, leaving wardrobes, beds and dressing tables, leaving pots, pans, ps, plates, glasses, decanters, knives, forks and spoons, leaving bed linen, towels and tablecloths, leaving hats, coats, shoes, socks, whale-bone corsets, nylons and suspender belts, leaving shirts, suits and ties, blouses, skirts, dresses and furs, leaving maids, leaving needles and thread, leaving shops and chemists, leaving restaurants, cafés, pin-ball machines and juke boxes, leaving cinemas, leaving churches, leaving newspapers, leaving factories, leaving farms, leaving garages, leaving offices with desks and typewriters, leaving medical practices, leaving hospitals, leaving schools and school-reports, leaving pet dogs and cats, leaving cars, leaving spanners and wrenches, saws, lathes, screws and nails, leaving pens and paper, leaving books and bibles, leaving memories, dreams and nonfulfilled diaries, leaving a half-white and half-green flag cut by a red crescent moon and star, flying victorious over Algeria the nation.

Now, despite the conveniences of the flat acquired by Azallah's uncle and aunt, they continued to spend most of their day among the squalor of Nador-Scala. The flat, yes, had five rooms, but each room had four walls, and each of them mocked them, jeered at their thin mattresses laid on the floor, ridiculed the small table, the mats, and the tiny cupboard. A European-style flat, the family soon realized, required European-style furniture. It required a settee, a table and chairs, beds raised off the floor, chests of drawers and carpets.

This required money. Hassan told Mustafa that he would

have to charge them a monthly rent for the shack in the bidonville. After all, he and his son Saʿid had built it, and Saʿid, soon to come out of hospital, deserved all the amenities of independent Algeria!

With the first of this rent, Hassan and Latifa bought a second-hand dining table and chairs. They decided that this was worth a family celebration, and showed it off with the pride of the parents of a first-born son. Then, with a sheepish grin, Hassan asked his father what he thought.

Said he, Hadj Ali: 'You want to walk like a partridge when you've forgotten to walk like a hen.'

Hassan gave a ghastly laugh, which his wife took as the cue to hurry the feast she had prepared, worthy of a wedding.

Hadj Ali stood by the table, and after bismillahs, took a plate of chorba, and then sat on the floor, with his back to the door, and with a spoon there ate from the bowl in front of him.

This spoiled Hassan's appetite, and soon he joined his father, and bade him and Mustafa to see the sea from the terrace whilst the soup was taken away, and the viands and couscoussou brought in.

Said he, Hassan: 'Ya baba! At the end of next week I'll be giving up my job at the fish market. I'm going to start work as an official at the post office. You look surprised, Mustafa? But you forget! My son Saʿid is a war hero! Now I have pull. I tell you, this job is just the start.'

Said he, Hadj Ali: 'Black is black: now it's been tattooed too.'

Thereupon, Mustafa had turned, and gripped the rail on the balcony, his eyes already on the Mediterranean, north . . . to France.

And enough of them and that, and with respect to Azallah, the day broke and a water-blue sky ran over Africa, the imponderability of the thread on the horizon the omen of the continent with its spectra of potential sealed in prisms, wrapped from the sun by anguish, and ribboned by exploitation. And the ship anchored safely at Annaba, at the harbour which penetrates the city and is watched over by giraffe-necked cranes—

'The town was once surrounded by jujube trees.'

Bi-llah. Hence the name, balad al-anaba, town of the jujube trees. Now—

'What happened?

Happened–?

'To the jujube trees.'

They were chopped down by France to free the approaches to the city, as their army was being picked off by the Kabylies with long-barrelled guns. A death preferable to the miasmas of the marshes where, I think I am right, one in thirteen of the settlers died in the first ten years of colonization, though young and hardy all. As for the garrison of four and a half thousand soldiers, up to one tenth died of disease each year.

And in this vein I shall fare on with a further note re the fettle of the warriors of France, and I use as the *locus classicus* the writings of Saint-Arnaud, who in 1841 AD, AH 1258, was already a major, and in command of a rearguard action in a march from Mostaganem to Mascara. And I quote:

Not for a general's epaulettes would I wish to relive those ten hours on July 2. Hardly had the firing ceased when stragglers began to drop out of the ranks by scores, by hundreds, from every corps and every regiment. I saw the most hideous scenes of weakness and demoraliza-

tion. I saw soldiers throw away their arms and equipment and lie down to await death, certain and dishonourable death. Forced to their feet, they stumbled on for a hundred paces, only to fall again, overcome by heat, worn out, weakened by fever and dysentery. In order to try and avoid me they threw themselves down away from the track, in the thickets, among the ravines . . . Many begged me to kill them so they should not die at the hands of the Arabs. I saw some of them clasp the barrels of their rifles in a voluptuous frenzy as they tried to place them in their mouths . . . Today, there is a horrible sirocco: the air is hotter than the mouth of a lighted oven. . .

But I lose my thread. Where was I?
'Giraffes.'

And patience, for Azallah had disembarked from the vessel, to be directed with the other passengers into a large warehouse, and the delights of a scramble for landing cards to fill, and then the crush of people at immigration. He sat and waited on a bench, and thereupon came a man with shiny hair parted, and a well-lined face, and asked Azallah to be so kind to write his card and entry permit for his Peugeot, and thereat let his documents show he was an Algerian emigrant resident in Brussels. And so there formed a short queue of similar unlearned men, and so Azallah all but became a scribe, and was last to show his passport. He then exchanged some French francs for Algerian dinars, a few and no more, the reason being that he intended to withdraw large amounts later, from an account he held courtesy of the non-convertible dinar, and a currency control of 330 francs equivalent for Algerians a-voyaging overseas. And thus he had given francs to certain visitors beknown to him in Paris for dinars deposited in his name at the Banque Nationale d'Algérie, at a switch of twice the official exchange. Wa-llahi! You look shocked, but some Algerians in France profit from even four or five times the bank rate.

'But Rahwun! You speak as if to justify this. It makes the Algerian dinar weak. People use francs to buy the things difficult to get here. Then these goods compete with ours. It's a threat to the socialist rebuilding of our nation!'

Al-hamdu li-llah! As I suspected, we have a patriot amongst us! Ya sidi, listen: each day brings its loaf.

So Azallah stepped out into Annaba, and turned past palms which sang in the breeze, and into the growls of traffic along the Cours de la Révolution, bordered by the frippery of five-storey arcaded white buildings. Dividing the boulevard a canopy of trees threw filigree shadows on the long band of compacted sand where here and there kiosks stood like light-houses beside archipelagos of tables and chairs. And he passed by a mother seated with her two children, slipping a spoonful of sorbet beneath the lace-edge of her veil.

Thereupon, he began to search for a hotel, trying to read the unfamiliar script of the Arabic: fa . . . nun . . . dal . . . qaf funduq: hotel.

Now, have you ever noticed how impossible it is to find a room in a hotel in this country? They all appear to be occupied by vital conferences, or long-stay guest-workers. And so it was in Annaba, and two hours passed whilst Azallah trod the streets, and his bag seemed double its weight, and he felt a tremor of panic. Whereupon, he found himself in a side road which opened to a small square, where parked in front of the café men milled around three or four parked cars, and some shouted names or held overhead hand-written signs: al-Djazair; Skikda; Constantine. Now, Azallah chose the first of these inter-city taxis to leave, by hap bound for Constantine. And he made up the fifth passenger, perched precariously near the gear-stick as the driver crunched into first with the mutter, inshallah!, and off they roared.

They had travelled mere metres when the man beside Azallah had tried to sell him a pair of denim jeans, its leather label a-branded with the logo I write before me in the sand:

Wa-llah! and by this time the driver had shifted his knee into every gear but reverse. The straggle of suburbia they sped by. A *feu orange* dangled from the rear-view mirror impotent with the turbulence which buffeted through the wound-down windows of the car. Azallah concentrated on the road ahead. They passed by a boy tugging a mule. A plain stretched southwards to a line of hills. In the distance was a deserted homestead. They drove south-west, climbing into more rugged landscape. The azurine sky became curtained with clouds, and a light rain fell on the windscreen, and Azallah sat mesmerized by the arcs of the wipers.

The driver plugged in a cassette, narrowly missing a petrol tanker as he did so.

Said he, the driver: 'Warda! Warda Eldjazairia!'

There was a ripple of appreciation from the passengers, who wound the windows up, as if in salute. The music began. The ensemble of violins, and cellos, tambourines, recorders, flutes and dulcimers was interspersed with clapping like the wind a-rustling through a forest of trees. And then came her strong and marvellous voice which smouldered in the air like frankincense.

And I have no more to say other than: Praise be to God, the Mighty, the Omnipotent, the Strong, Eminent in power, the Creator of the heaven and the earth, and of the land and the seas!

'Ya Rahwun: that cannot be all which you relate! What has become of Siddiq?'

Perhaps he is worth a few more douros than you have all thought fit to donate. Meanwhile, I give you this to guess:

A tree of God has five branches;
Two are always in the sun, and three always in darkness.

Sahha! But what has prompted today's generosity is a riddle in itself!

The Fifth

Wa-llahi!

Nearly a week has gone by since my wife took the children to visit her family in Touggourt. The house is as silent as death: how I miss the squabbling of little daughters as they decide who will open the door to me; how I miss the smile of my wife. And the nights are a torment of solitude. Meanwhile, I know that the mother-in-law will revile me as she feeds her daughter such platefuls that I can only hope that, inshallah, she will not die under the spoon.

So were you suitably foxed by the riddle I posed last week, or would you like a little clue? Perhaps if—

'Ya Rahwun! I think that the tree of God is prayer—'

In the name of Allah, the Compassionate, the Merciful!

From the minarets of Constantine, five times a day, the cry of 'Allahu akbar, la ilaha llah, Muhammadun rasalu llah, hayya ila s-salah . . .' still floated, ethereal, over the choppy terracotta sea of roof tops, to invade streets, alleyways, cul-de-sacs and courtyards, to cross thresholds, steal through windows, and spiral into the cochlea of the inner ear to spark the nerves to the brain.

Five times a day.

The altar and the crucifix, a regiment of chairs, the heady mists of incense and the stains of candle flames on the air, had transfigured the mosque of Suq al-Ghazzal to the cathedral of Notre-Dame-des-Sept-Douleurs.

Yet the muezzin's calls to prayer confronted the tricolour.

Five times a day.

Siddiq had watched a military garrison built, the kasbah. Buildings had been razed to open squares. He had seen wider straighter streets speared through the maze of Constantine's veins, designs to comfort the Europeans and intimidate we Muslims, and to allow the rapid deployment of troops.

Yet still, still, still.

Five times a day.

Houses damaged by battle or broken by age were collapsing, or falling into disrepair. Constantine had become a calamity among calamities, her face appeared pitted by smallpox and slashed by long scars, and her mouth marred by rotting teeth. And her masters watched their captive shrew, unwilling to encourage her rejuvenation, and lo, one by one her buildings began to be sold to or expropriated by her captors for a fraction of their worth. The Commissaire Civil of Constantine, Lapaine, had designs to not only allow the free settlement of Europeans, but to establish the city as either an agricultural, commercial or industrial centre, and a missive to that effect was sent to the Governor-General of Algeria, the autocratic Thomas-Robert Bugeaud.

Now, he was known as Père Bugeaud to the French (for his deeds, his benign moon-face, or both?) and in their nurseries children would puff on their toy bugles the chorus of the military song sung:

L'as tu vu',
La casquette, la casquette.
L'as tu vu',
La casquette au per' Bugeaud?

The English called him the Butcher of the Berbers. Amongst us, he was nicknamed the White Haired Warrior, and was as true a thorn in the flesh of Abd al-Qadir as Abd al-Qadir was to Marshal Bugeaud.

'In death as in life, ya Rahwun! In the capital the Place Bugeaud has been renamed the Place Emir Abd al-Qadir!'

Naʿam: it seems, my friend, you know Algiers quite well.

Bugeaud, yes, was the true conqueror of Algeria, though his methods were as shocking as his officers found his predisposition to speak of manure, ploughing instruments and livestock. He wrote, and I quote:

In Europe we don't wage war against armies, we wage it against interests. When we have beaten belligerent armies we seize the centres of population, of commerce, of industry, customs, archives and soon these interests are forced to capitulate. There is only one interest to seize in Africa, agriculture; there it is more difficult to take than elsewhere, because there are neither villages nor farms. I have reflected on this for a long time, as I get up and as I go to sleep: well! I have not discovered another means to subjugate the country than to seize this interest.

And he did, and the campaign between Miliana and Cherchell shows how, if you allow me to cite some extracts from the correspondence of Saint-Arnaud, and treat them with respect, for he is already a Lieutenant-Colonel.

5 April 1842 *We are among the mountains between Miliana and Cherchell. We have fired few shots, but we are burning all the douars, all the villages, all the huts. The enemy flees before us, taking his flocks with him.*

7 April *The Beni Manacer's country is superb . . . We have burnt everything, destroyed everything. O the war! The war! How many women and children, seeking refuge in the snows of the Atlas, have died there of cold and misery . . . Our casualties were five killed and forty wounded.*

5 June *We lay waste, we burn, we plunder, we destroy the crops and the trees. As for combat, little or none; just a few hundred or so of wretched Arabs who fire on the rearguard and wound a few men.*

1 October *When I last wrote I was among the Brazes. Now I am among the Sindgads. The same thing on a grand scale . . . A few tribesmen brought their horses as tokens of submission. I refused, because I wanted a general submission, and began burning once more.*

5 October *Here I am with my little army, burning the douars and huts of the insurgents, raiding their silos and sending to Miliana the*

corn and the barley that I draw from them . . . I shall leave them in no peace until they submit.

18 January 1843 *I shall not leave a single tree standing in their orchards, not a head on the shoulders of those wretched Arabs . . . Those are the orders that I have received from General Changarnier, and they will be punctually executed. I shall burn everything, kill everyone . . .*

8 February *On the dispatch of the Governor [Bugeaud], I began the march to rejoin him in the mountains. On the 4th I reached Haimda. I burned everything in my path and destroyed the pretty village but it was impossible to proceed farther . . . when day dawned we saw that two foot of snow had fallen . . . No sign of a track, nothing; just snow, more snow. I started off, and I had hardly made a few hundred paces, what a sight. . . . the war seemed to me hideous. Heaps of bodies huddled together, frozen to death during the night. They were the unfortunate population of the Beni-Naaseur, whose villages and huts I had burnt, who I had driven before me . . .*

O Saint-Arnaud! Tragedies indeed for the soldier who so valued luxury and boasted one of the finest tables in Algeria thanks to the chef he had coaxed from Paris, six years in the employ of the great restaurant *Au banquet d'Anacréon*. O . . .

But I am beginning to drift. Now, the White Haired Warrior believed in the domination of us, 'The Arabs', as the prime objective in Algeria, and his preference was for military rather than civil colonization. And thus a letter sealed the fate of Constantine.

Bugeaud replied to Lapaine, writing that in his opinion Constantine should be neither an agricultural, industrial nor commercial centre. It was to be administrative. He demanded that the military took control; that a separate European quarter be delimited; and that outside these limits no European settler would be allowed to purchase, rent or build property.

To do so would risk the cancellation of the deed of purchase and expulsion from the city. Moreover, the best compensation was to be paid for any Arab property expropriated, and the reconstruction or repair of existing property should be encouraged.

Whereupon, this was all enacted in the *Moniteur Universal* at the end of one spring nearly seven years after the conquest of Constantine. The city that was was partly preserved, yet the restrictions on property sales imprisoned the Algerians therein, whilst new European quarters spread all around her like a coarsely woven haik.

And though church bells might ring, the human voice still swelled over the city.

Five times a day.

Allahu akbar, la ilaha llah . . .

The room was one-two-three-four by four-five-and-a-bit paces across grey and white reconstituted marble tiles veined with cracks of misuse and wear. A light-bulb dangled from the loftiness of the ceiling, its weak jaundiced light softening the edges and corners of the room with shadows and patterning a wall with the curves and angles of an iron bed-head. The wall opposite had a window with two frames which swung inwards and rose high, two panes in each chestnut frame; a jagged hole ventilated the top left, the glass was crazed on the bottom right. A third wall was broken by a door and a plugless porcelain sink, its single chrome tap crowned with the letter F: an emblem of coldness: an evocation of France. The fourth wall was bare.

Azallah sat down on the rough grey blanket tucked round the mattress of the three-quarter-sized bed: springs groaned at decades tied to the ephemerality of the traveller. He rubbed his hands together to stimulate the circulation, occasionally cupping them to receive the warm turbulence of his breath. Just an hour before, tendrils of panic creeping through his body in the drizzle-laden darkness he had found this, seemingly the only available room in Constantine, at twenty dinars a night, in the Hôtel Sahara.

. . . la ilaha illa llaaaaaa!

Presently, the rasp of metal against spinning stone roused Azallah from a sleep of turbid dreams. It was 7 a.m. His nose was pinched by cold, his breath condensed, and the natural light through the uncurtained window bathed the room with textures of greyness. A breath, and he threw back the covers of the bed. The floor was icy beneath his feet. He removed his T-shirt, his teeth chattering with cold, and he soaped and splashed water under his arms and over his face. He dressed and ran his fingers through his hair. His electric razor hummed competition with the machine outside. He splashed on a liberal dose of cologne. He frothed gel toothpaste over his teeth, scooping water from the tap to rinse his mouth. Blood from his gums tinged the spittle he washed down the drain. He wiped his mouth with his towel, which he draped over the bed-end to dry. He opened the window. It gave straight across a narrow cul-de-sac to a blank wall which rose above two bolted shutters set above a waist-high band of tiles, their blueness and floridity not quite obscured by the spatter of dirt from the street. The once-white paint over the rest of the façade was patched with stains and faded red curls of Arabic graffiti. Looking up, Azallah could see an oblique rectangle of sky; below the lane was paved with flagstones laid in chevrons and a middle-aged man with a club-foot angled a knife edge, and a stream of sparks flared heavenwards from a motor-driven wheel.

He pulled on his anorak and left, locking the door with an elaborate key. A black stencilled 2 identified the door which terminated the passage that dog-legged off the long landing doubling, by means of a chair, table and calendar, as a reception to the hotel. Louvred shutters opened from the other bedrooms onto the corridor. From somewhere came the sound of sloshing water.

Azallah left the hotel via a narrow flight of stairs down to a courtyard, whereupon he turned into a street with an incline which distorted perspective. It was lined by three or four storeys set over shops, their wares at that hour concealed behind rolled down metal shutters. Flooding sun from a lazuline sky quickened the white icing Montmartre façades of the west-facing buildings, and obscured the easterly with pewter shadows. The flag of Algeria folded from a pole angled from a first-floor balcony. People milled on the pavements and road. Youth outnumbered the old. The brown burnous and white turban, the black haik and white veil, were submerged by the large-collar kipper-tie flared-trousers platform-footwear bygones of Western fashion. The air was crisp and sweetened by the rain of the days before, and by the promise of the warmth of the day to come.

At the top of the street, where several roads merged into a reach of tarmac and the sky burst open from the hems of buildings, Azallah arrived at a café, its plate-glass windows rectangled round from a narrow frontage to the depths of a lane. Outside he added 1 dinar 50 centimes to the avalanching pile of coins beside the newspaper vendor who sat hunched beside three or four stacks of papers. He took a copy of *El Moudjahid*, and for the benefit of my friend if he is here today, he took the French-language version, its black title underlined in red printed with white: La Révolution par le peuple et pour le peuple.

'Sahha!'

Inside the café was heavy with the pungency of ground coffee and cigarette tobacco. The tables were packed, and all was enlivened by the tock-tock, drone and hiss generated by the espresso machines. Azallah walked to the rear of the long L-shaped room, its dark wood and rich hues accented in black and in places, above the dado, lightened by mirrors, their silvered backs spotted and tarnished.

A waiter in a burgundy jacket, his hair oiled, slid a cloth over the table, and took Azallah's order, *wahid qahwi wa croissant.*

A stumpy china cup: the coffee arrived, a bare mouthful of ebony liquid encircled by caramel-coloured froth. Into it he broke four blocks of sugar from the aluminium bowl on the table. The croissant was gold encrusted and its layered inner flesh milky. He turned the pages of the paper, finding the news factual and the articles rose-filtered through the maxims of Third World socialism. Under the section *Culture*, there was a full-page article on B——, martyr and hero during the War of Independence. The scars, O brothers, ran twenty years deep.

Azallah counted his money, placed it on the table, and strolled out through still-crowded tables, passing a child selling biros, and out into the street and the throng and a plaza with views to the right, and a theatre and post-office to the left. The buildings ended abruptly at a small park where sand paths twisted between low-fenced flower beds, whilst opposite, across the wide road, the cordon sanitaire over two mass graves divided the city into the former Muslim quarter behind, and the European quarter ahead. A girl, her hair pulled under a scarf, her dress flowing, flowered and spread around her, sat with her hand cupped upwards and her eyes puckered over sightless eyes. Azallah descended into an underpass, set with small booths selling perfumes and carousels of postcards: scenes of Constantine, plump Caucasian babies in baths, romantic sunsets backdropping silhouettes of lovers. Up into the daylight to the Place des Martyrs, and the glass frontage of Air Algérie, the customers therein outnumbered by friends and family to oversee the purchase of tickets to exotic possibilities in Algiers and Cairo, to religious fulfilment in Mecca, to a life in Paris, Lyon or that grisly city Marseille. Azallah followed the curve of the pavement, passing the Hôtel Cirta opposite, and turned on up the Rue Abane Ramdane past blue and white tiled shops, their counters covered with trays of date lozenges and coiled and twisted fritters drenched in syrup, and half-heard was the sizzle of oil within. He crossed over to walk uphill beneath arcades, dawdling past the shop frontages of a past age and culture. He wandered into a bookshop, its air fusty, its walls lined with half-empty shelves, stocking some books on French jurisprudence, some books in Arabic, and a few copies of André Malraux's *L'Espoir*. Thereupon, he continued on to the top of the hill, where the roundabout of Place du Colonel Amirouche was centred with a small obelisk surrounded by four cannons. He turned, passed a bubble-on-a-stick telephone box, and took a street where the pavements were set with trees in front of low white buildings with shuttered windows, and intricate iron balconies. Faded red, blue and bleached white awnings sloped from the shops over vegetables piled in wooden boxes outside, and shaded a window chequered by record covers too.

Sunshine mellowed the air, and the road swept Azallah

down and on impulse he turned off and descended a narrow lane of steps which led to a road falling westwards. A Renault with French number-plates was parked by a gate half ajar which led to the apex of the European cemetery. Azallah wandered ahead along an avenue lined with marble tombs and granite gravestones, and here and there stone angels perched as if petrified on the instant of flight. Scattered cypress trees spired to the sky. Glass-fronted black and white photographs of a man and his wife stared across the weeds to a slab cracked in two which bore the name FAMILLE GRELET. Whereupon a voice shouted, and Azallah hurried away startled as a hooded ancient in a burnous hastened towards him. A black crow screamed as he neared the gate, and flew across his path, and Azallah's heart pounded and he began to run and only paused for breath some distance away.

Panting slightly, he arrived full circle at Air Algérie and recrossed the Place du 1 Novembre 1954 where a road rose to the pretty Hôtel de Ville, and where Western façades masked the soul of the Algerian city behind. He wound into the hive of buildings where the pavement barely allowed the passage of one person, and the street was but one car wide, and, passing sheep skulls grinning from a window, he returned their smile. He stopped at a bakery, its window half-filled with vertically-stacked baguettes like sentinels of history. In a doorway a turbanned man balanced on metal caps strapped on to severed thighs, and Azallah was reminded of his cousin Saʿid's endless days, packed in his wheelchair on the balcony of the flat in Diar al-Mahsul in the capital.

Presently he veered into a tiny shop, and bought a piece of khbizer sʾmina, cut in a parallelogram from a large circular tray, wrapped in paper quickly transparent with grease. The semolina soaked in sugar syrup, fragrant with orange-flower water, was a morsel of childhood. He moseyed on by restaurants opened to the street, selling liver or lamb brochettes, cram-packed and noisy with customers. From a urinal further on an old man stepped out and buttoned his trousers; then Azallah passed a garrison gate and groups of students coming and going clutching briefcases and books and folders. Then in front was the Sidi M'Sid suspension bridge which spanned the ravine, and it seemed he crossed a catwalk cat-cradled from the sky, zigzagging women in veils and a single line of oncoming cars.

On the other side he climbed steps along a cactus-fringed path, passed grazing sheep, and turned down to an Arc de Triomphe which framed the eternity of the sky. Beyond was a sundial and map etched in bronze and the name Cycle Club de France.

His senses seemed sharpened to a razor's edge. He no longer looked through clouded panes. As if for the first time he smelt, he heard, he felt. He was alone, standing at a balustrade atop a cliff which fell to a rolling green landscape hung from a great blue sky. He breathed deeply, the candy air filled his lungs. Complete stillness: he was alone, standing at a balustrade atop a cliff which fell to a rolling green landscape hung from a great blue sky.

You seem restless, habib-i. But some things have to be said. You seem restless, so let me whisper to you one word.

Women.

'What about women, Rahwun?'

'Ya Rahwun, you cannot stop there.'

So I have captured your attentions. Yet a horrible haze seems to have obscured my memory . . .

'Ya Rahwun, perhaps this one-dinar coin will be sun sufficient to burn the mists away?'

Wa-llahi! My memory is returning already!

Aywa, and I was about to comment, are not Algeria's womenkind remarkable? Just one young lily, Marium Ben Atala, who amazed by her beauty everyone who beheld her, and enchanted the eye of everyone who saw her and more, inspired Pierre Louÿs as he wrote the *Chansons de Bilitis* in Constantine. Does she not breathe in these extempore verses?

> Upon a white terrace, in the night they abandoned us, swooning like roses. The warm perspiration slipped away like tears from our armpits over our breasts. Overwhelming voluptuousness purpled our thrown-back heads.
>
> Four captive doves, bathed in four perfumes, fluttered above us in the silence. From their wings, drops of perfume fell upon the naked women. I was covered with an essence of iris.
>
> O lassitude: I rested my cheek upon the belly of a young girl who enveloped herself in the cool of my moist hair. The perfume

of her saffroned skin intoxicated my opened mouth. She closed her thighs around my neck.

I slept, but an exhausting dream awakened me: the inyx, bird of nocturnal desires, sang distractedly from afar. I coughed with a shiver. Little by little, a languishing arm like a flower raised itself in the air towards the moon.

O rub me down with ice! The ersatz of which is to continue, and hence I give you this, a name.

Jamila.

The frown of one of you says, 'My wife?'

La, not your wife!

Then perhaps Jamila Boupasha? The young Algerian girl arrested near the close of our War for Independence for throwing a bomb into a café in the capital, and who lost her virginity, not between the white linen of lavender-scented sheets entwined with a loved one, but by the thrust and twist of the neck of a bottle in one of the torture cells of the French army.

La, not our martyr and heroine, Jamila Boupasha.

Another.

She was born in Setif, in the very same year that the Prime Minister of France, Léon Blum, and a former Governor-General of Algeria, Maurice Violette, tabled a plea to enfranchise twenty-five thousand of six million Algerians, by granting citizenship without the renunciation of their statutory right to Islamic law, and envisaged further an evolutionary process to political assimilation with France. And with these coals the colonial machine thrummed and rolled into action to protect the threat to its supremacy, its cogs and gears actuating the lobbying of Parliament, and manipulating press campaigns in Algeria and in France, and pushing *anciens combattants* to protest through the Paris streets, all in all delaying the plan two years, until Léon Blum's Popular Front was replaced by the right-wing government of Daladier. Thence the project was dismissed by the French Senate, without discussion.

And so Jamila grew up during the Second World War, the war when France was a model to her Commonwealth, and crept into a corner like a kicked dog, and sulked a little before wagging its tail as the Nazis goose-stepped down the Champs-Elysées. And Jamila was nine, and the war was over, and Fifi barked victory whilst the pied noirs bedecked their buildings with flags and pennants to celebrate VE Day, and their triumph over fascism. But ho, the celebration in Setif was marred by the audacity of the melons, ratons and bicots who demonstrated for their own freedom with cries of *Long live Algeria, Free and Independent* and *Down with Colonialism*, and for the first time waving the green and white standard of Abd-al-Qadir, now our national flag. And a stone was thrown, or a shot went off, and five days of craziness and frenzy ensued as protesters against the *présence française* fanned out into the countryside and Europeans were killed wa-llah, you could count one for every year of colonization. And there followed a backlash of butchery by the armed forces, the chance to use us as the whipping boys for France's humiliation by the Third Reich, with summary executions in profusion, and villages bombed by Douglas dive-bombers, and days of terror and confusion. And lo! forty-five thousand Algerians were massacred in the weeks following VE Day, and this tally included the mother of Jamila.

Thereupon it was back to business as usual for colonialism, and leaving Jamila to cook and clean and wash clothes and wipe the noses of her younger brothers. Then, two years later, we Algerians were given citizenship with the title of French Muslims! And five reforms, namely, democratically elected local councils, the suppression of military government in the Saharan territory, the recognition of Arabic as an official language alongside French, the separation of religion and state for Muslims, and, let me grab a breath, electoral enfranchisement of Muslim women, were five reforms blocked by a medley of intimidation, falsification and ballot-box stuffing, thus keeping the Algerian Assembly firmly in the hands of the European minority.

Jamila cooked and cleaned and washed clothes, and no longer wiped the noses of her younger brothers, but suffered their screams and insults and smacks and beatings instead.

Now, you know the proverb: he who cannot take a hint cannot comprehend a long explanation, and so it was that the War of Independence began. And Jamila was eighteen, and her seventeen-year-old brother arrived home in Setif in a blizzard one night a prop to a stranger who clutched at his shirt all sodden with blood, wounded in combat against France in the countryside a few days before. Whereupon they made the young man, they knew not his name, a bed and Jamila tried to clean the deep wound of its grit and its dirt. Her father sallied forth, and from one pharmacy to another he traipsed, begging medication but to no avail, for France had placed antibiotics, ether, alcohol, and anti-tetanic vaccine under an embargo which required we Algerians to identify ourselves and our patients fully. Presently the wound became purple in hue, and the skin around it swollen. The young man burned and shivered, and his face became skull-like, his skin olivine, and his eyeballs protruded, and Jamila wept for he had such beauteous brown eyes. And so-and-so murmured the name *Nadia*, for he thought the girl bent over him his sister, for her beauty was like charming flowers, and he fleeted between the bitterness of winter and the embrace of summer, and his head was filled with the granite staccatos of sub-machine guns and intumescent images of fire. And Jamila stayed with him as the poison excreted by the bacterial cells voyaged through the bloodstream to the spinal cord, as he sweated, as he was seized by cramps, as his teeth became fixed in a grimace, as his body flew into violent contortions and arched with but his head and his heels touching the mattress. His legs and his arms were flung in every direction in a manner mad and wild, then he lay paralysed, and then again his legs and arms were flung in every direction in a manner mad and wild, then he lay paralysed, and then his legs and arms were flung and his breathing became laboured and it stopped, and it was over.

From the dead youth's neck, Jamila removed a deer-skin talisman, and hung it around her own. Moreover, his death touched off a toxin which had lain latent in her blood.

Said she, Jamila: 'Ya baba, I must join the fight.'

Said he, her father: 'Your family needs your help!'

Said she, Jamila: 'Ya baba, this country needs my help.'

Said he, her father: 'I have just come from your aunt. Your brother Hamid is to be married in the spring to Fatiha, and so they will live here. You should taste her couscous! Wonderful, as light as air, and not one grain bigger than another. And so the time has come when we can find you a husband, inshallah! Your aunt is already combing the city for someone suitable, so put this nonsense about fighting out of your silly head.'

Said she, Jamila: 'I refuse to marry a man I haven't met. If my brothers can join the revolution, so can I.'

Said he, her brother Umar: 'You show neither shame nor respect. You dare to talk like that to your father's face?'

Said he, her father: 'This house is cursed! You cannot show yourself outside without your veil. You will be called a whore! Do you want to bring dishonour to your family? What have I done to be punished like this? If you leave this house now, you leave for ever!'

Whereupon Jamila turned, and walked out the door into the street, and in her new status joined the maquis, which sent her for service in Constantine.

Now, Jamila had pale olive skin and the features of a Southern European and her first role in our struggle was this. She dressed in knee-length skirt and a short-sleeved blouse above the elbows, and she walked from point to point across the length and breadth of Constantine, suffering the leers of gendarmes and militiamen, but she was able to return their smiles because of the grenades and guns and explosives variously concealed within her bag.

O sons of Algeria! You made your decisions and you left to fight, exchanging a hoe for a gun, or relinquishing the tedium of your city job for the excitement of battle. It was not so easy for our daughters, such as Jamila! The veil and haik and ankle-length dresses had disciplined, isolated, and comforted her body. Without them, Jamila felt that she had been hacked into pieces, that she floated and had very nearly dissolved, and that her limbs grew and grew and that she stood quite naked in the street. And she had to learn to walk in an unnatural manner to escape detection, using measured easy steps with her shoulders thrown back and her hips swinging and yet . . . not draw attention to herself.

O sons of Algeria: by comparison it was easy for you.

Alack: I sense a sourness and rising hackles around. Thus far concerning Jamila, but as regards Siddiq, know, O my brothers, that the year after the conquest of Constantine the

Ben Nassif family had returned from Tunis in a state of utmost joy and happiness, with the addition of a baby boy, Khalid, to the family of three girls. And Siddiq was rewarded for he had saved the house and the heirlooms within, and he stayed and became a companion to this son.

Six years passed until a summer when the city was like a furnace which dried the saliva from the mouth, and young Khalid fell ill with a mysterious swelling on his leg and a violent fever. His father wept and pressed the child to his bosom, and the women rent the air with their wailing, for they knew not what to do to save him.

Now, Siddiq went forth to the mosque and performed afternoon prayers, and there he heard that the marabout Si Abd Allah was on a sojourn in the city, and this was fortuitous indeed, for Si Abd Allah was renowned for his skills with medicine. Such tidings: and lo, a messenger was sent from the Ben Nassifs to the marabout.

'A few douros for our story-teller to help break his silence!'

'A few douros more and he'll break the bank! I have a cheaper way. Ya Rahwun, let me give you this to guess:

Greener than grass,
Redder than meat,
Thinner than gruel.'

Ya habib, the answer can only be a fig—

'So you are silent no more. Here is another dinar to tempt you to continue, inshallah!'

Sahha! Great knocks on a wooden door, a noise like thunder-claps shook the house, and the marabout Si Abd Allah was ushered in. He was tall, with a square face and eyes with the colour and brilliance of sapphire and a nose as true as a sword and a red beard like a burning bush. He carried with him the leaves of the prickly pear, and bunches of ground-pine, and he wafted with the spiced sweetness of resin.

Said he, the father of Khalid: 'Happiness hath betided us by thy coming.'

Whereupon Si Abd Allah requested the use of the kitchen and there he placed the leaves of the prickly pear between hot ashes. In a small cauldron he boiled the lobe-leafed yellow-flowered herb down to a liquor and poured it into a silver vessel. This he fed to the sick child, and then applied the hot leaves to the swelling on his leg.

That done Si Abd Allah took himself to the corner of the room and performed his prayers, and thereupon clicked his way through a rosary of ninety-nine amber beads chanting three times thirty-three of 'Subhan Allah' and 'Allahu akbar' and 'Il-hamdu li-llah'.

Then Siddiq and the marabout sat with the boy throughout the textures of silence which mark the passage of night—

'—and story-telling—'

—until Siddiq began to shift with restlessness, until he

swallowed deeply, and summoned courage to address the marabout.

Said he, Siddiq: 'Ya sidi, I will say to thee some words and I will await your counsel. Some time ago I had a vision of a giant nest on a precipice, so I came to this city, Constantine. But I also had a vision of flights of birds and schools of fishes and a terrible cyclone. What does it all mean?'

Now, Si Abd Allah was inly a-startled, and he looked at Siddiq, at his sad eyes and full lips, and at his hair tightly plaited in ridges against his scalp, and he walked twice across the room, and then he spoke.

Said he, Si Abd Allah: 'From time to time I give a guarantee of safe conduct to persons of my choosing who wish to wayfare through the Kabylie. And oft beyond. This is known as the anaya.'

Said he, Siddiq: 'Of this I have heard tell.'

Said he, Si Abd Allah: 'Then you will know that the anaya is the Sultan of the Kabylies. It is inviolable. For a time it places people outside the law and the ill will of their enemies. Until now proof of my support has been shown by means of this stick. These bands of brass are inscribed with verses from the Holy Qur'an. Your visions, il-hamdu li-llah, have led you to me. If you wish, you may leave the employment of the Ben Nassif family to accompany me in my daily life. And as and when necessary you may act as the material sign of my anaya by escorting and presenting people to the marabouts of successive Kabylie tribes.'

Said he, Siddiq: 'Inshallah. Once the boy is well the Ben Nassif family will need me no more.'

Said he, Si Abd Allah: 'But one day one will need me.'

And by dawn, Khalid's swelling had subsided and his fever had broken. God is bountiful indeed!

And it fortuned that Khalid begot a son who begot a son

who begot a son who begot a son Bashir in the year of the centenary of French Algeria, when it seemed that nothing would change and all that had passed was the first hundred years of a millennium.

And Bashir spent his childhood in the enjoyment of comfort and ease and repose, and on the occasion of his circumcision he was given a Series Hornby clockwork train, its 4–4–2 tank locomotive in the black Etat livery, its Pullman carriages brown, its goods wagons in a profusion of cheerful colours, and it ran around a large circle of rail till stopped at a tin-plate station, with clip-on names of Dijon, Lille and Nantes, where little lead figures of a gentleman traveller, a lady tourist, a cleric and a station master stood by tin trunks affixed with Paris labels.

Now, whereas many Algerian families as illustrious as the Ben Nassifs sent their children to a French lycée and then on to a university in France, Bashir was sent to the medersa of M'Sid for a Qur'anic education, and to a private tutor, Monsieur Grelet, to learn French. At twelve he was sent to the Zitouna mosque in Tunis to be schooled in rhetoric, metaphysics, theology and grammar, and from there he was sent to al-Azhar University in Cairo to study jurisprudence. And that was the year Israel proclaimed itself independent, the year that the Zionists set about their programme of expulsions and atrocities and massacres so as to seize Palestine and scrub it clean of Arabs, ever reliant on their single-word apology, 'Holocaust', and the weakness of America. And each day this repression continues, my eyes still cry, cry tears of blood.

But I wobble from my track towards a quagmire.

Hh-hem.

Then four years later Bashir thrilled as Egyptians en masse rose in protest, for British tanks had fired at point-blank range on police barracks in Ismailia murdering forty-one. A madness erupted in the streets, and symbols of the hated allegiance of pashas and foreigners were buildings burned and wrecked, and a thick mantle of smoke hung over Cairo marking Black Saturday and just six months to a coup d'état, and the abdication of King Farouk.

So it was, his studies complete, and the pilgrimage to Mecca and Medina performed, that Hadj Bashir returned to Algeria in the summer our combat began, and he travelled from Algiers by bus through towns and villages where the pieds-noirs played boules in dusty squares, or drank pastis in cafés beneath shady trees, and shop signs read Épicerie, Boulangerie, Pharmacie, and such, and the names of rues, avenues, and boulevards tended to celebrate the literati and the military of France. And he thus arrived in Constantine.

Now, his family wept for joy and his return was whiter than the face of day. His father bade high festival held, and there followed a great abundance of eating and eulogy until Hadj Bashir was asked of his plans, and he cited his intention of joining the National Liberation Army, whereupon his father went puce and clutched his heart.

Said he, his father: 'Now is the time to think about marriage. You are my only son. What if you were killed tomorrow? Who would be the guardian and provider for your mother and your sisters? What of all the money I spent on your education? Let me sit down, I have shooting pains like daggers in my chest. I shall die an unhappy man! Let others fight the battle for you! If they succeed your role is certain: to help the élite construct a new nation.'

Said he, Hadj Bashir: 'I must help now. This is our country, and the pieds-noirs must leave.'

Said he, his father: 'There are two types of pieds-noirs. Yes, there are the bad-willed, the ones who accept the inequalities in this society and ensure its continuation by force. But there are also the good-willed. For example, Monsieur Grelet, your French tutor. He was always mentioning the economic, political, and moral scandal of colonialism!'

Said he, Hadj Bashir: 'In Egypt there is the fable of a hunter and a sparrow. A hunter was hunting sparrows one cold day. As he killed them, tears rolled down his face. One sparrow said to another: "There is no danger from that man. Do you not see him weeping?" The other said to him: "Do not look at his tears. Look at what his hands are doing."

'Ya baba, the good-willed and the bad-willed are one. The good-willed find the structure of society unacceptable, but they continue to enjoy its privileges. The only ethical course of action is for them to go. For myself, the only ethical course of action is to fight.'

So he went, and for his initiation he was told to kill and so prove his reliability, and thereupon bind him as an outlaw to the ALN. And during this task he would be shadowed and he himself dispatched if he so much as hesitated in the deed.

Now his subject was a *mouchard*, for the striplings amongst us, an Algerian police informer, so vile that he doomed many men to vanish in the torture cells of Constantine at the Cité Améziane, and was a person such as the poet hath described:

> He is a dog, a dog's son, and a dog was his grandsire;
> and no good is in a dog, the issue of a dog.

And lo, on a black night in the old town, Hadj Bashir grabbed the wretch from behind and slit his throat with a razor as with a sheep at il ʿid or the ritual sacrifice towards the end of the Hadj. And he tied the whelp to a metal post in the Rue Sayid Ben Tchicou, and set his right arm in a French army salute.

Then, at the maquis, Hadj Bashir beheld Jamila, and he lost his reason, and his mind was captivated and his heart was entangled in the snare of her love as her heart was in his, for fires had shot into her heart on his account, for he was a perfect man of four-and-twenty carats, fair to the sight with eloquence dight, and a mole on his cheek-breadth like an ambergris-mite, and eyes as black as plums.

In war the future hour is uncertain, so they were married by special licence. And they spent their wedding night in Room 2 of the Hôtel Sahara where, putting off their clothes, Hadj Bashir and Jamila stood by the bed and sought love-liesse. And his mouth pressed on her lips until he drank her honey-dew and she thrust her tongue like a tit-bit of meat between his teeth. Hot lust stirred in him, and they tumbled on to the bed, and he held her tight to his chest and his hand slipped down between her thighs and his pizzle stood at point like a huge key, and he breached the lipped entrance to the citadel and became lost in the darkness therein, and Jamila cried the cry of heavenly mysteries as a fountainhead of milk gushed forth in a moment that was enough to make a man forget his father and mother and war. And in the early morning they were serenaded by a young lad with a club-foot below their window, sharpening knives on a motor-driven wheel.

And soon after, Destiny issued her decree, and Hadj Bashir was arrested in the street, outside a café grilled against grenades, and he looked from what was then the Place Nemours across the lively Esplanade de General Leclerc below the Hôtel de Ville, and a blushing sun slid through a lemon sky. He stood, his hands behind his neck whilst the militia searched him. It seemed that the sun and the sky had the redness and yellowness and fluidity of wine. Voices yelled. Hadj Bashir stared at the sunset, his head swam as he stared at the sunset. He drowned in the sunset . . . and the light was fading and the temperature was dropping, and Azallah Boudjemaa leant on the balustrade before the Hôtel de Ville looking over the empty esplanade to see pearl-grey smoke billow gently from a city rubbish tip which spilled down a hill, whilst a blushing sun slid down a lemon sky. Whereupon the street lights and building lights started to flick on to touch the dusk with a glimmer of magic.

And now my wits have fled me and need some fillip to return next week – shukran! Wah! My leg is cramped: can someone help me up?

'Ya Rahwun! Are you to take your leave without setting us a riddle?'

Bi-llah! So there are still some who do not find my conundrums mundane? Then I give you this to guess:

My beast is yellow;
one does not relish its milk;
and one does not eat its meat.

Glory be to the Living One who dieth not and in whose hand is the dominion of the worlds visible and invisible!

The Sixth

Last night my brother talked me into going to the cinema. No, he assured me, not to see some twenty-year-old Italian film with subtitles, some Egyptian extravaganza, or even an American Western, but an Algerian film, *Umar Gatlato*.

So some of you have seen it! I dislike these ends: did he rendezvous with the girl or not? I trust that was the end, as the film was constantly distorted by the projector. Or maybe I missed something as the soundtrack crackled, and each time a woman was profiled on the screen the cinema erupted with whistles and cat-calls. But my concentration was not at its best, as my seat wobbled and creaked, my neighbour spat by chance on my foot, and there wafted a fulsome and loathsome smell from the toilets.

The film was good, I agree, but I recommend to those who have yet to see it to hold on till it appears on television.

In the na—

'Ya Rahwun! Min fadlak! The answer to the riddle!'

The answer to my riddle?

'It must be a mother-in-law?'

'Ya Rahwun, you're laughing! Is he right?'

Not quite, though the answer was a scorpion. And know that I know one is amongst us now.

Hhem.

In the name of Allah, the Merciful, the Compassionate!

Jamila heard nothing.

She and Hadj Bashir had moved to the house of the Ben Nassifs shortly after their marriage. At first she was greeted coldly and with contempt: where was her trousseau, her négligés, gold-embroidered dresses, other raiment, dish-cloths and towels? Twenty or so suitcases full would have melted the ice, five might even have cracked it, but none! But Hadj Bashir said naught. Then his mother wept and wailed and tore at her hair and encouraged her daughters to follow her example, whereupon his father waxed and waned about his dicky ticker and threatened palpitations, and in a lull Hadj Bashir broke the news that Jamila was carrying his child. Felicitation replaced lamentation and Jamila was received with open breast and merry favour, whereupon cous-coussou was steamed with raisins then crowned with dates, sweets and hard eggs, and accompanied with platters of fowl and viands of a varied and tempting appearance. Then Jamila was almost fussed over, and later had the benefit of advice and an unctuous smile from her father-in-law.

Said he: 'The Ben Nassif family is a family of honour and dignity. A young bride has no reason to leave the house except to visit her family and the hammam, and this you will remember, inshallah!'

The former option was impossible, but with a baby due, and anxious to please her husband's family she smiled yea, certain that independence was not really far away.

Then, alack and alas! One week later Hadj Bashir was arrested.

And Jamila heard nothing.

She went into labour and gave birth during that morale booster for the FLN, Suez. And just as that forty-hour 'war' was a disappointment to France, so was the addition of a girl to the Ben Nassif family.

And Jamila heard nothing.

She nursed the baby, whom she named Zubayda, and her in-laws considered it time that she should keep herself occupied, and rustled her up a routine: mopping the floors, airing the bed-linen and then to the matter of great importance: what should she cook for their lunch?

And Jamila heard . . . nothing.

Wah! And Azallah Boudjemaa and his family arrived in Paris at the time when Paul Delouvrier, the former Delegate-General of Algeria, unveiled the grandiose Schéma Directeur to halt the asphyxiation of the Ville Luminaire with five new towns, schools, hypermarkets, theatres, express métro services and urban ring roads. And in this alien universe, where it was cold and damp and the skies were low and grey, Mustafa stumbled about until he found a job on the production line of the R10 at Renault to which he left early and returned late to the shanty town where they lived. And there their first European winter was spent between board walls and a mud floor living in fear of fire and vermin, and frequently unfreezing communal water taps. And Azallah and the other boys kept warm by endless games of football, setting four jerry-cans on the sodden earth for the posts. And so they fared until Nadia became brazen with ambition.

Taking Azallah as her translator, she went to the authorities to present her case for a flat, and the reply was a shrug and outspread arms and the promise of one soon. As they left Nadia turned to Azallah.

Said she, Nadia: 'Remember this proverb: a promise is a cloud, only a deed is rain. We shall return again, and again, and again.'

And again, and again and again they did until finally, for her family, she surrendered the last of her pride before an astonished official behind the desk, and cried. The first few tears were sham pure sham, but then they would not stop, and Nadia wept endless tears wrung from a bruised and secret heart, tears for her first-born son Moktar, allah irahmu!, tears for her missing brother, tears for the dust and the stones and lost bird song of her Kabylie village, and tears for the heat of the African sun.

Al-hamdu li-llah! The official was new to the job and still soft as dough, and two weeks later Nadia moved her family into the two-bedroom flat in the concrete orgy of Courtillières, at the eastern, antiquated end of the estate. The building had five floors; their flat was on the fourth, and a French family had lived there before. It had a balcony and a double aspect, facing north-east–south-west. No one cared there was no east-facing entrance. And the block was fronted by bare earth, where boys played football or lounged around in gangs. Behind was an unfenced railway line leading to a factory. There were shops and a school near by, and a walk beyond passed the complex which was the longest dwelling in France, meseemeth to have been squeezed from a giant rectangular-nozzled toothpaste tube, and was a snake to the western zone of supra-quality tower blocks, of landscaped greenness, and fewer foreigners.

Nadia kept the windows covered with curtains, for she could not look out when she had lived her life on the ground. She carried her memories like a head of hair, sometimes lank and tangled with neglect, increasingly discoloured with age, though daily brushed into a shining cascade before being suppressed and protected by a scarf. Yet all the while, single strands fell unnoticed, invisible and abandoned.

And their manner continued, for Nadia still rubbed her teeth clean with black ash, and she and her daughters ate by the cooker in the kitchen, while her husband and son ate apart, facing the door in the lounge.

The new world that Mustafa had embraced left him with a void he knew not how to fill. He spoke French with muddled tenses, syntax, and declensions, and poor rhythm and intonation, all peppered with slang and obscenities learnt on the factory floor. Nevertheless, he insisted that everyone spoke French at home, but Nadia, for the first time in her life, refused to obey her husband.

Said she, Nadia: 'Arabic is the language of God. My children will never blush with shame at my spoken word.'

Whereupon she kept her integrity, albeit brief, for during the drama and the dazzle of the May 1968 uprising, she started to speak hesitantly in a queer and quirky French, words spawned by a terror of being isolated by her family.

Azallah was placed in a remedial class at school, and lived in dread of Madame le Censeur, a pied-noir with hands like pitchforks, and a mouth like a dark cave and teeth like pebbles, and eyes like a fish, who wreaked her lust for the lost voluptuousness of the skies and smells of Algeria on the North African children in the classes she kept strictly in check. Anxiety spun Azallah into a cocoon of voicelessness, and at times he would have the hazy memory of watching the boys at school in the village where he was born, scratching slate pencils on boards as they wrote, in a script free and flowing, various verses from the Holy Qur'an, and hearing the musical chant as they repeated them under the direction of the maellem. Then the clang of a bell brought him to the present, and he emerged, aflight with wings of radiancy.

Late one night Mustafa arrived home, red-wine pixilated and fou as a coot. Above them, below them, on both sides of them there came the boom and quaver of radios and televisions, and the voices of neighbours. He yelled at everybody. He demanded his supper. Nadia pulled it from the oven, flung it in the sink and turned on the tap. Mustafa punched her once, and as she reeled, twice again. She collapsed to the floor. He swore at her in French. He kicked her, and then struck a blow at Azallah as he tried to pull him away, and thereupon Mustafa fell to his knees and wept like a tiny child.

Nadia lay very still. She could taste the blood as it trickled from her nose. And she smiled.

Thus far concerning them: but as regards Hadj Bashir Ben Nassif, he had been taken to the Cité Améziane on the western fringe of Constantine, and led therein to a semi-darkness spiked and torn by screams and hoarse cries and someone's desperate plea of 'Vive la France!' And Bashir was ordered to remove all his clothes, and his hands were handcuffed behind his back, and he was prodded into a vertical grey box which forced him to stand, or to sit cramped or twisted up against its wooden walls: but what more comfort could he expect from a polling booth on loan from the Hôtel de Ville? Then the room was plunged into darkness, and a door thudded shut. But wa-llahi! Despite all this cunningness, the day and the night were never one, for, ingrained by the regularity of daily prayer, Bashir did not lose track of time. So it was in the early morning that a key clicked in the lock, and the light would glare, and he would be let free to be drenched by a hose jet of ice-cold water which gushed until his stomach turned blue, then yellow, then mauve, then black. Then the jollity and glee of the teenage paratroopers would redouble as Hadj Bashir was fed his daily morsel, which with his hands handcuffed he had to eat from the bowl on the floor like a dog.

Then darkness.

He thought of his unborn child, and he thought of Jamila, and he thought of their well-being in the womb of his family. And he was eased as he mentally recited verses from the Holy Qur'an . . . *The present life is like a golden globe with which the earth bedecks itself when watered by the rain. Crops, sustaining man and beast, grow luxuriantly: but as its hopeful tenants prepare themselves for the rich harvest, down comes Our Scourge upon it by night or in broad day, laying it waste, even though it blossomed but yesterday.*

A key clicked in a lock. Doors were thrown open, and from a silhouette at the entrance came the order: 'Number 582! Out. Hurry!'

Poked on by a truncheon, Hadj Bashir was hurried along a length of corridor punctuated by the moans of men, and then half-tumbled down a flight of stairs to a large cellar.

Said he, the paratroop captain: 'Dieu et Muhammad, laisse-les dehors. Ici c'est la France. Now sit in that chair, and listen well: you will tell me the names of your comrades in the National Liberation Army, and then confess to your crimes against France. So soon: already you refuse to co-operate? That is a pity, but maybe my friend here will help you to change your mind. This flex has been insulated so well that your teeth cannot bite through it. This end is bare, and plugs into this socket on the skirting, like so! Now at this other end here is a thin plywood tube, kept very damp to allow the maximum amount of electricity to pass through. And from these two bare wires . . . but you are intelligent for an Arab. Look, Sergeant! I'm not sure what is quivering more: these two wires or this bicot? Now if you wish to make conversation, you have only to lift a finger or a foot. No? Then I hold your nose so, and down it goes . . .'

Whereupon Hadj Bashir jerked as the wires were pushed into his throat, and the current clamped his jaws and clenched his teeth, and through flickering eyelids the world was reduced to lightning which seemed to tear him asunder, and to flashing geometric patterns of green, red and blue, and he was left with the thirst of one who had been ten days in the Sahara without water.

Said he, the paratroop captain: 'Sergeant, disconnect please. Bring me a piece of tape. My friend: you refuse to come. So, I pull out this wire, thus, and Sellotape it to the end of your penis, so. Handy they're all circumcised, isn't it, Sergeant? Now remember, you have only to lift a finger or a foot. Sergeant: if you please.'

Bashir jerked upwards, before him spun wheels and whirlpools of light spiralling into a vortex of unquenchable thirst.

Then blackness.

'Then . . .?'

I too am consumed by thirst. Perhaps if someone could fetch me a mint tea with six sugars from the café over there, my tongue might become moist enough to continue.

'Ya-llah!'

'In this heat?'

'Well don't dally!'

'. . . and do you know the price he asked for that goat . . ?'

'That's cheap compared to ten eggs!'

'If you can find them—'

'Ya Rahwun, I have another riddle to give you, inshallah!'

If you must.

'Two kings on a carpet: one has an army and the other has not.'

The Moon with its battalion of stars, and the Sun. Wallah: my tea! Shukran, habib-i.

Shhhhhhhhhhhhhh-p: that's better.

And through the blackness flew birds and fish of all kinds and colours, and presently Hadj Bashir came to, cramped once again in his box, and before him floated the vision of a great serpent brooding on its eggs, and of scorpion fighting scorpion, whereupon his mind reeled with these verses from the Holy Qur'an . . . *And in the land there are adjoining plots; vineyards and cornfields and groves of palm, the single and the clustered. Their fruits are nourished by the same water, yet we give each a different taste* . . . A key clicked in a lock.

Said so-and-so: 'Number 582! Out! Hurry!'

Down to the same cellar room.

Said he, the paratroop captain: 'I do apologize. It seems that the methods of persuasion I use on my friends leave them very thirsty. Now, if you wish to speak, just lift your little finger whilst you have this drink of water. Sergeant.'

Shhhhhhh-p.

The sergeant nodded to two adolescent paratroopers. They hauled Bashir to a trough of water and forced him to the ground. The sergeant seized a hand of hair and thrust his head in. Hadj Bashir kicked like a mule, but only rubbed his knees raw on the concrete floor.

Whoooosh!

He gasped for air.

Splash.

Hismotherhisfatherhiscircumcisionthecryofyouyouyouyou trainandMonsieurGreletTunistheTurkishcoffeehousecandle lightandshiningbrassawomansprawledonabedandpyramidsan dtheviridesenceofpalmsandtamarisksandacaciasandeucalyptu satAlFayummarblecolumnsarcadesandthelibraryofAlAzharm osquethebluenessoftheRedSea . . .

Whoooosh!

Huah huah huah hu—

Splash.

JuttinglatticewindowsinthetallhousesofJeddahdesertMecca roundroundroundroundround round roundkissingtheblacksto neheat 'labbayka'llahumma labbayaka' night under a host of stars casting pebbless having heads the green domed mosque of Medi na the Radiant Jamila knife across a throat through a liquid sunset into . . .

. . . darkness.

Shhhhh-p.

Light. *The life of this world is but a sport and a pastime.*

A key clicked in a lock.

Said so-and-so: 'Number 582! Out! Hurry!'

Said he, the paratroop captain: 'I am sorry for you. I see how tired you are. However, I am happy to inform you, on behalf of France, that the Government has no wish for you, an intellectual, to lose your life or rot in a cell. They want you to live and work as a free man. Unlock his handcuffs! Give him clothes to put on!'

Shhhhhhhhhhhh-p.

And lo, it was night, and Hadj Bashir was driven until the sky was coloured by the sunrise, and the jeep passed through the guarded gates of a farm. There, he shared a room, and slept on a bed, and he was allowed to wander about but never alone, for to be himself was tantamount to rebellion and likewise silence was forbidden. Thus Hadj Bashir could make no impression on the environment, rather it seemed to penetrate him and lay quite leaden upon his heart. Time became measured by the seasons and the sun, and whilst spring became summer and summer autumn and autumn winter, Hadj Bashir and his companions were given a chance to engage their brains.

First, he had to make statements on the value of French heritage and the merits of colonization. In order to perform the task as well as possible a French sociologist, a French psychologist, and a French historian were ever present to prod the lackadaisical mind.

Second, Hadj Bashir was presented with the arguments for the Algerian revolution and asked to overthrow them one by one by a display of silver-tongued intellect and conclusions which averred:

> Algeria is not a nation, it has never been a nation, it will never be a nation!
>
> There is no such thing as the Algerian people!
>
> The revolutionaries are ambitious peasants, criminals, and poor mistaken creatures!

Whereupon rewards were awarded, no one knew how many for what, nor how many were few, or how many a lot, but on their tally lay freedom. So if Hadj Bashir had a misgiving he guarded it, for otherwise he would have jeopardized progress he had made, and worse still, at times he suspected that perhaps his jailers were right.

Then, one day, he was told that he was to be set free. This procedure was well kenned: at the start a seminar in which collective criticisms were crowbarred ad lib, upon which hums followed haws till with regret liberty was regretfully postponed

Yet, al-hamdu li-llah, Hadj Bashir was freed! And he returned to Constantine, and lifted baby Zubayda in his arms, and Jamila and his family wept abundant tears as all his physical loveliness had fled in consequence of the severity of the horrors he had endured, and they trembled at his fear to switch on a light or touch a trilling telephone. And then his family and his comrades gathered to congratulate him and rejoice, for he had held out and compromised nothing nor no one, and now once again he could join in our glorious national struggle!

It was at that moment that a terrible doubt laid the seed of disease in his mind.

Perhaps he had not deceived anyone but himself?

Know, O my brothers, that eleven full moons had come and gone, and Siddiq had travelled sans surcease through the smiling hamlets and perched villages, and deep valleys and the rugged mountains of the Kabylie, and even far beyond, and autumn had frozen into winter and winter had melted into spring, and summer raged. And Siddiq had been the anaya to a holy man, to a poet from Baghdad, to a murderer, and to a vizier, and he had also served as the escort for an arcane Englishman en route to meet Emir Abd al-Qadir in the Ouarsenis.

Now, the marabout Si Abd Allah requested that Siddiq accompany a certain sheikh to be presented to the assembly of notables of the tribe of the Sbeah from the Dahra Massif, to the west of the Kabylie. And their peregrination reached a close as they strolled up through a hillside forested by mighty elms and oaks, which wove an ethereal shade and cast dappled shadows glinting with ice-diamonds of sunlight, and around them birds warbled with various tongues, proclaiming with the sweetness of their notes the perfection of God, whose name be exalted!

Said he, the sheikh: 'Ya Siddiq! Tell me of the Emir Abd al-Qadir, for I have heard that you have met him.'

Said he, Siddiq: 'The Emir is small of stature, and has a face which is long and pale, a beard which is black and bushy, and eyes which are blue. His hands and feet are small and exquisitely formed, and indeed he pares and files his nails in a coquettish way with a small knife with a mother-of-pearl handle. His skull caps, shirts and burnouses are plain with no trace of gold or embroidery.'

Said he, the sheikh: 'But then does he not say that nothing enhances the dazzling whiteness of a burnous better than blood?'

Said he, Siddiq: 'Yes, and yet there is an air of melancholy gentleness about him. I think it best if we ford this brooklet here. The Emir's elocution though is brilliant and lively and words and ideas pour into his head like cream into a churn. Here, let me help.'

Said he, the sheikh: 'Sahha! Brr, that water is as cold as Satan's heart!'

Said he, Siddiq: 'Now, I recall that the Emir spake this which I tell thee: Take a thorn bush and for one year water it with rose water, and it will not produce anything but thorns. Take a date palm, leave it without water, without cultivation, and it will always produce dates.'

Said he, the sheikh: 'Wa-llah! And let me say this: France can chew us and chew us again, but they will never swallow us. Since France infracted the Treaty of Tafna, the resistance of the Emir has been heroic. We've watched as four years ago his capital Tagdempt was captured and destroyed, and as successive defeats chased him over the Moroccan frontier until last year, when the victory of France at Isly chased him out again. Yet still he and his partisans return to fight. The White Haired Warrior, I have heard tell, says that the strength of Abd al-Qadir lies in his elusiveness, the vast distances traversed for battle, the heat of the African sun, in the lack of water and the nomadism of the Arabs. But I am of the opinion that his handicap is the disorganization of his troops, who will not sacrifice their tribal loyalty for national sentiment. France calls him an ambitious fanatic;

Christendom a visionary adventurer; and Islam a hero saint. What say you?'

Said he, Siddiq: 'Time will decide, inshallah. But I myself revere him as a poet.'

And seeing a wild boar snuffling some way ahead they thought it wise to pause, and sat themselves on the trunk of a fallen tree, and Siddiq recited these verses by Abd al-Qadir composed on that delightful city Tlemcen, commencing thus:

At sight of me, Tlemcen presented,
for kissing, her hands white and sweet,
my conquering arms, above her hips,
encircle her, and love tempts me!
I shall remove the veil to her noble figure,
my heart palpitates with joy,
and her cheeks glow like flames.
Her mouth resembles the Ring of Suleman,
and corn opens on the surface of her skin
making down upon my hand!
What enemies have died from her pride,
what lovers, zealous of her beauty,
wishing to rape or ruse or compel
her cool gardens, such sensuous bait!
But her gaze is steeped in contempt,
killing them, beneath her haughty ramparts,
her eyelashes lower to my smile alone,
does she give me the kiss of a lover?

Said he, the sheikh: 'Sahha! Well let us hope that the Emir does not suffer the fate of Embarak, allah irahmu!: after being killed by France in battle at Oued Malah, the White Haired Warrior had his head hacked off and salted and served up on a salver at a soirée for the entertainment of his guests.'

Said he, Siddiq: 'Inshallah!'

And then they fared on, and soon found themselves where they had intended, sore exhausted for stress of hunger and fatigue, but alack-a-day and alas! the village was in a state of mayhem, confusion and capsizal, for France had been sighted marching fast upon them. So Siddiq and the sheikh had little alternative other than to join the men, women and children as their hearts quaked and they hurried from their homes and their agriculture and other employ to escape the clutch of their pursuers, and seek refuge in the windings and the intricacies of the grottoes a stone's throw away.

Now, the troops intent on this razzia were led by a certain officer, then a colonel, of which you know: Le Roy de Saint-Arnaud.

'Ya Rahwun! Go on!'

O brother, I cannot, for my heart will shatter like a clay vase.

'Here's a dinar for a pot of glue.'

'And another!'

'And these.'

'And this!'

Shukran! I shall continue.

Siddiq and the refugees settled in the depths of the caverns and the only sounds were the echoes of the cries of a babe.

Whereupon there came a call for the tribe to leave the caves and surrender.

Shots from a rifle were fired in defiance.

Night was closing. Saint-Arnaud paced, though he knew exactly what to command, for Bugeaud had written two months before: *if rebels retreat into caverns, smoke them to the bitter end, like foxes*. Whereupon, a Colonel Pelissier had done just that to seven hundred souls of the Beni Ouled Riah.

The order was given. Fires were kindled at every entrance to the grottos, bar one aloft, and they were fed sedulously with wood, bracken and grass until the night stars seemed their very sparks, and soon they roared louder than any cannon as a wind drove thick smoke in wild, whirling eddies into the mouths of the caves.

But the brave Sbeah still did not surrender.

Saint-Arnaud strutted back and forth, unsure of the solution for such stubbornness. Worse still: piqued, his subdivision of troops were all a-mutter, for were they to withdraw and leave the tribe free, to mock or gleefully gun them down like rabbits, or run a knife across their throats?

Meanwhile the fires burned until the dawn reddened softly for mankind, and then alone Saint-Arnaud entered the caves.

Thereupon, inspired by the civil outcry against the *modus operandi* of Bugeaud and Pelissier, Saint-Arnaud determined an answer which had the advantage of veiling the deed.

The order was given. All entrances were to be plugged with rocks and stones, leaving the bodies therein interred. Then leaving the cemetery behind him, Saint-Arnaud was later to write this: *From the 8th to the 12th, I have been ill, but my conscience does not reproach me.* I have done my duty as a leader, *and, tomorrow, I will do the same again. But I have developed a distaste for Africa.*

Amongst the expressions of the five hundred dead, had he

noticed the face of the grandfather with the Qur'an in his hand; had he noticed the faces of the young men, if not stern as iron, puckered with hatred, or stricken with despair; had he noticed the faces of the dead mothers weighed upon with love for their families; and had he noticed the face of Siddiq, as he nestled a child in his arms?

We can only speculate; we will never know.

Now, here it would be lethal to linger more, and I shall recount a tale that has reached me from the tides of yore and ages long gone before. It concerns one of the most celebrated musicians of the city of Constantine, Muhammad, who was called upon to play in every festival and feast, and each time his skill was rewarded by showers of gifts.

However, he too was stricken by a death: that of his newly married son who had shown every promise to inherit his father's talent and reputation. Now, the old man never ceased to ask the Prophet, may Allah bless him and grant him peace, to let him live long enough to pass on his knowledge of music to his only grandson. And wa-llah: this child, Ahmed, showed a true passion for music and all things melodious, and the old man had him a flute made specially to fit his small hands, and took him to festivals, and it soon became apparent that his talent would rival that of his grandfather.

One day, the child was left alone in the house, and upon returning Muhammad was surprised, nay startled, to hear music played by two instruments. Thinking that another musician was a-visiting, he quickened his step, but lo! on entering the courtyard he saw only the boy, and he alone was producing this sound.

Now, on examination it emerged that the lad had inserted his little flute into his grandfather's, and hence it surpassed the range of the latter by an octave. And when questioned further, he replied simply that he had wished that his voice follow that of his grandfather.

Whereupon, marabouts were summoned to pronounce on this, and concluded that the Prophet, may Allah bless him and grant him peace, wished to indicate that the boy would continue the reputation of his grandfather, and indeed, exceed him in excellence.

And so it was, O my brothers, that the flute was called djauak: literally, that who follows.

Hh hem.

And so to Modern times, when several thousand quavering voices said: 'We turned this beggar girl into a princess. Let's leave her as we found her.'

And thus Algeria suffered the final humiliation of colonization, as she was shorn of her sequins and satin and jewellery and apparel by the far-flung destruction of buildings, bureaucratic records, machinery, communications, infrastructure, et cetera, and by the flight of her cadre of doctors, dentists, executives, engineers, teachers and more to boot.

Nevertheless, Algeria held her head high, independent and free.

Then the FLN became the single party of our nation, and Ahmed Ben Bella our first president. Do you recall his speeches, you must, stewed up from a cookbook of radical Marxist theory, always garnished with Trotskyist overtones, and sweetened with sugar-drops of Islamic socialism. And how appetizing the air smelt with the various aromas of Collectivization! Co-operatives! Workers' self-management in industry! State control of the agricultural sector! And equality for all!

But ho! The father of Hadj Bashir Ben Nassif had lost his sense of smell and thus had no taste for such cuisine. He thrived instead on his own regimen, viz. the acquisition of land and enterprises for a token of their worth as the pieds-noirs took fright and fled, and this included a villa in the plush and leafy residential suburb of Bellevue, and to there his family moved lock, stock and barrel from their house in the ancient quarter of Constantine.

Now Hadj Bashir politely declined to join his father and brothers-in-law in the mini-renaissance of the Ben Nassifs, and decided instead to practise jurisprudence. However, a comrade from the FLN prevailed upon him that he could best help the new Algeria within the corridors of the civil service.

Bi-llahi! And there Hadj Bashir watched, as, into the vacuum left by the Europeans, war veterans and loyal members of the FLN hurried and hustled, pushed, scurried, and scrambled, for the lack of a lusty entrepreneurial bourgeoisie meant that the only way up the ladder was through the ranks of a) the administration and b) the Party. And Hadj Bashir watched as the civil service became peopled by moudjahines, some literate and waving a primary school certificate, others chuckle-heads or illiterate but able to brandish scars, or the odd epic story from their exploits in the struggle against France. And Hadj Bashir watched, as their days began late and finished early and spanned a lengthy lunch, and were otherwise broken for breaks for coffee and—

'Ya Rahwun! My brother works with SONACOME. Last year a co-operant arrived from Eastern Europe. He was allocated a desk, and told that he would be seen some time later that morning. After two hours he was ushered into the director's office. There, the co-operant expressed his distress, and stated that whatever the issue, he voiced his solidarity; however, he could do nothing more as his contract forbade him to participate in strikes. Wah! The director looked puzzled, and said: "What strike . . . ?" '

Naʿam. So it was that Hadj Bashir's mind seethed with squiggles of question marks which asked whether he had been offered this job as a penance or as a reward? Perhaps . . . perhaps They were convinced, or even knew, that he had collaborated with the French. Perhaps . . . perhaps he had been brainwashed after all, and thereby was a perfect tool to help replace the colonial bourgeoisie with something as like as two dates? Perhaps it was a trap? Was he trapped? Perhaps, perhaps . . . perhaps.

Then, three years after Independence, our country once again confronted its Destiny, with the swift and bloodless coup d'état by the Minister of Defence and Commander-in-Chief of the National Liberation Army, Houari Boumédienne. Wa-llah! We are all familiar with his famous proclamation:

People of Algeria . . . From now on verbal socialism is dead; the building of a socialist economy has begun. Future generations will not remember the words, they will judge the acts.

Thenceforth Algeria embarked on policies of state capitalism, and the single-minded pursuit of centralism and industrialization, all. And acronyms abounded to herald the new state enterprises:–

SONITEX	SN SEMPAC
ONALAIT	OFLAE
SONATRACH	SONELGAZ

And on building fronts and through the streets banners read:–

AGRARIAN REFORM MEANS SOCIAL JUSTICE

THE PEOPLE BELIEVE IN THE LEADERSHIP

SEEK THE TRUE ALGERIAN CHARACTER
THROUGH THE CULTURAL REVOLUTION

Now, Hadj Bashir thought them, no, knew them to be mere socialist pap behind which a new bourgeoisie was ever strengthening its control. He thought that, no, knew that this hungry quest for capital-intensive industrialization did little more than to help to enforce a powerful and wealthy bureaucratic élite.

Of which he was one.

And lo! Gaps between forecasts and achievements continued. Income distribution and employment suffered. Bureaucracy creaked. And each day from the window of his office Hadj Bashir could see a streamer fluttering with the words:

THE ALGERIAN REVOLUTION CONTINUES

And this prompts me to finish with this riddle. I give you to guess:

> It is a stone of the river, and it is not a stone;
> It is embroidered, and it is not a handkerchief;
> It has four feet and it is not a sheep;
> It lays eggs and it is not a hen.

Shukran! Such beneficence: I am almost overcome. Were it that these dinars were gold!

And now Praise be to the Requiter of every good and evil thing, the Lord of Majesty and of Kings the King!

The Seventh

Al-hamdu li-llah! My wife and children are back, and with them they brought this story which I shall recount.

One day a jackal arrived at a farm. The cock heard him, and to draw his attention away from the hens, he ran and perched in a tree.

Said he, the jackal: 'Are you not my brother? Come and pray.'

Said he, the cock: 'How can you pray? You must wait for the Imam.'

Said he, the jackal: 'Who is the Imam?'

Said he, the cock: 'He's a saluki, and he's coming.'

Said he, the jackal: 'Pray, for it is time, and my ablution is not yet done . . .'

Said he, the cock: 'I'll wait for you.'

Said he, the jackal: 'Pray with me now, for one can only find water two to three days' journey from here.'

Wa bi-llah! Neither cock nor hen, jackal nor saluki is the answer to the riddle I posed last week, though that hint should suffice.

Guess or I'll beat the lot of you with my stick!

'Is it perhaps an exotic bird?'

Do birds have four feet?

'Is it a tiger?'

Do tigers lay eggs? But if you know the value of letters, this animal does begin with a 't'.

'Tarantula?'

'Is it a tortoise?'

Allah yitawwal 'amrak! I only wonder how many of you could win a race against it!

In the name of Allah, the Merciful, the Compassionate!

Now with respect to Azallah Boudjemaa, it was one Friday noon, and the mosques were so packed that the faithful performed their prayers outside and down the steps and in the street. And Azallah surged into an alleyway in the ancient quarter of Constantine which he did not know, and it burbled with a torrent of men. Here and there they huddled into obstructions towards the wall, heads bobbing nods, in a conspiracy of grins and leers one to the other. He was prodded into one tight little eddy which swirled in front of a low door pierced with bars. Behind this he glimpsed a shadowed room in which a woman oozed ample and fleshy and avoirdupois from elephantiasis. He drew away, but the current threw him across to another vortex, protected by a counter, behind which two girls sat, one with a hand of six fingers and the other with two foreshortened arms. Azallah meandered on, then veered sharp left, and took refuge in a doorway. Beside a table by him stood sentry a hefty dame, her lobes beneath her scarf stretched by earrings into a savour of Emmenthal. Instinctively he dropped a few coins into a chipped saucer, and was pointed upstairs to where a long corridor gave off to several rooms and a courtyard roofed by a rose skylight set in by intricately fashioned wood, and thereat stood a short queue of men waiting at the first riser of a narrow staircase. A door opened; a man came down with a smile stretched goopily across his phiz and made a show for all to know that he zipped shut his flies. For the stairs led to Heaven and the star of Constantine!

Presently Azallah ascended. The room he entered smelt of cheap perfume, of carbolic soap, of the tang of citrus fruit, and sweat and recent sex. A grey and white kitten played with an oblong of orange peel beside an ornate and mirrored wardrobe.

Now a shaft of light from a high window flooded obliquely on to the girl as she reclined on the bed and her hair was as black as the feathers of an ostrich, and her eyebrows were thick and arched above eyes as green as jadeite, and her teeth were like pearls set in native gold, and she reclined ready in a gossamer gown with which she toyed as she told Azallah in French to clean his prickle at the sink. Whereupon he undid his trousers and lathered the soap, then turned towards a chair to lay his clothes.

Yeeeeee-ow!

Azallah tried to avoid the kitten which streaked right before him, tripping and losing his balance and falling forward to knock his head against the edge of the bed end. The girl leapt from her mattress pose as playmate. Azallah gave a moan. From beneath the bed she pulled a first-aid box, and helped Azallah sit up. The sheets smelt sour and scrambled his stomach as she wiped the small swelling gash on his forehead, and he winced as she painted it red with acriflavine.

Said she: 'Are you all right?'

Azallah nodded, and asked her her name.

Said she: 'Yamina.'

Time was passing, others were waiting, he had to go. She began to rub her fingertips in soft spirals around his navel until he stood with head erect, and she lifted his hand to stroke her breasts but lo! he held her wrist and said, no more, whereupon something invisible and strange fluttered between their hearts with the lightness of a butterfly, and Azallah was overcome, and on impulse spoke.

Said he, Azallah: 'Can we meet?'

Said she, Yamina: 'It is forbidden.'

So, Azallah stood up to leave, and belted his jeans, and pulled his wallet from his jacket and counted out five ten-dinar notes and laid them on the bed.

Said she, Yamina: 'Outside the station, at ten tomorrow morning.'

Azallah went to the door and down the stairs and wa-llahi: the men below looked at the wound on his brow with boggle-eyes, and in their excitement all but foamed at the mouth and swooned.

Now, O my brothers, another legend, for I am in the mood to recite all manner of myths today. Have you heard of the Beni Meriin?

'The language of thunder . . . ?'

'The kings of Tlemcen . . . ?'

The one, and also the other.

Kan ma kan. In olden times, and in an ancient age and period, the Kings of Tlemcen had dealings with fallen angels, and worse still, their ally was Satan. And by casting sand on a black table, they were able to foretell the future.

Now, one day, one of the Beni Meriin espied a maiden drawing water from the Oued Tafna, and, verily bewitched by her, he desired her for his own, and love gat hold of his heart like a fire. But what a vanity, so certain was he that the merest of nods would acquire her as his slave! However, the girl was pledged to a warrior of her tribe, and thus chose to ignore this Beni Meriin and all his bonny cajolery.

Thereat the world waxed black before him and he flew into a rage, and swore to himself that he would revel in the tears of this nymph who refused to bestow on him even one of her cherry smiles.

So the King waited until the girl went forth from her douar to meet her beloved beneath some palms, and then called upon the Devil to aid him. Whereupon Satan seized the two young people, and dragged them down into the bowels of the earth.

Instantly, the luxuriousness of the landscape was transformed, and the fertile valleys of rainbow flowers were replaced by scrub and the silver-blue of the olive tree. Only the palm remained, marking a clear-water spring filled by the relentless tears of the lovers who remain imprisoned underground with the Evil One as their warder.

But enough of this; and as regards Jamila Ben Nassif—

What is all this commotion? Has a jinn materialized in your midst?

'Let me through. Ya Rahwun! I bring from your family the terrible news of the death of your father, allah irahmu! You're wanted home at once.'

The Eighth

'Is-salamu ʿalay-kum.'

'Wa ʿalay-kum is-salam.'

'No story-teller today?'

'No. We've already been waiting a while, but he hasn't shown up.'

'Unusual for him, isn't it?'

'Didn't you know? His father, allah irahmu! died last week.'

'And I heard that Rahwun's brother has come from Paris.'

'And another from Qusantina.'

'You mean Constantine!'

'Wa-llahi!'

'Didn't Rahwun work in Qusantina too, at one time?'

'He taught history at the university, but then, for one reason or another he came back here—'

'—and worked for a while in the date factory out at Le Souf. Packaging. Then he left. Suddenly.'

'And now?'

'He comes here once a week to entertain us.'

'It all seems odd.'

'Doesn't it?'

'So Rahwun's still in El Oued?'

'Inshallah! I've just fixed his typewriter for him!'

'French or Arabic?'

'French, why?'

'It could be of use. I'd like to know how he manages to live off story-telling.'

'He must have a patron!'

'Perhaps that's why he needs his typewriter repaired.'

'*Well—*'

'Well I'm off to the café. You're all gossiping like women. Rahwun is a most kind man. He tutored my son in English, and refused to accept even a douro in fees.'

'I'll join you.'

'Sahha! We'll see you next week.'

'Inshallah! Ya habib, what did you mean when you said "*Well—*"?'

'Aren't you a stranger to El Oued? Nothing. I meant nothing at all.'

The Ninth

Remember, O my brothers: God endures, all else passes away.

In the name of Allah, the Compassionate, the Merciful!

Now, Jamila stood siege from her mother-in-law for not bringing forth a son or sons, and at night the she-devil spied through key-holes and listened at doors, then alone together in the day shouted abuse and intimated divorce and was rude, rude, rude, wholly unaware that her beloved Bashir had been returned fixed and phobic about physical contact if disrobed and quite nude. Then deadlock, and then retreat as she began to concern herself with the marriages of her own daughters, and as their first-born sons simpered and cooed. And otherwise she spent the rest of her days at the cemetery, or visiting local marabouts, or going to the hammam, after leaving instructions for Jamila to mop and dust and beat carpets and prepare dinner and wash mountains of clothes, and Independence came . . . and went.

And Jamila stood by an ever more distant Hadj Bashir, and loved and brought up Zubayda, and bided her time and waited for a sign that white days were near. Whereupon, one morning she soaped and scrubbed and wrung and rinsed the laundry, and the radio was on, and there sounded the tones of an arpeggio, *d de dee deee deeee . . .* and the charismatic voice of Ahmed Ben Bella, President of the Republic, filled the room and spaketh thus:

'The Algerian women, who played an important role in the revolution must play the same role in the construction of our country. We oppose those who, in the name of religion, wish to leave our women outside of this reconstruction. We respect Muslim traditions, but we want a revolutionary Islam and not an Islam left to us by colonial domination.'

da daa daaa daaaa daaaaa . . .

'An attempt has been made to place the Algerian woman behind a screen to prevent her from doing her duty – to participate in the life of Algeria. Women should be mobilized like men to build a happy future for the country. It is not the wearing of a veil that makes us respect the woman, but the pure sentiments we have in our hearts.'

And Jamila almost wept and hugged the radio, and ran to unfold one of the dresses she had worn whilst smuggling arms for the maquis and pulled it on, and walked out thus from Bellevue to the city centre. And thereat men gave her lewd and obvious looks and someone behind her asked to see her pussy, and another commented loudly on her tail. She ignored this all. She walked into a café. There was a momentary hush, and she found a place and she sat down. The waiter avoided her. She waited. Then the man at the next table leant over with a half-smile.

Said he, so-and-so: 'When are we going to fuck?'

Two other men turned round too.

Said he, so-and-so the second: 'How much do you charge?'

Said he, so-and-so the third: 'I've already screwed her silly in the toilets for free!'

Said she, Jamila: 'You filthy bastards!'

Said he, so-and-so the second: 'Who are you calling a bastard?'

And Jamila quit the café, and hurried back to Bellevue, and she vomited, and she tore off her dress, and she washed herself twice from head to toe, and thereupon returned to the washing, and told herself, too soon, too soon.

And three years slipped slowly by and Jamila was peeling vegetables with the radio on and in this wise came a speech of the new President, Houari Boumédienne:

d de dee deee deeee . . .

'Women already have rights they had fought for and should not, therefore, demand them. Women could drive tractors if they wished—'

Said she, Zubayda: 'Ya umma! It was so funny at school today—'

Said she, Jamila: 'Not now!'

Said she, Zubayda: 'Yes, now. Listen, I want to tell and I will!'

Said she, Jamila: 'Let me listen to this, and then you can tell me. Please.'

'—there exists the problem of unemployment: when a job is available

should it go to a man or a woman? Should the man be left at home while the woman is permitted to work? That is the problem.'

da daa daaa daaaa daaaaa . . .

'Emancipation of women does not signify imitation of Western women. We say "no" to this type of evolution for our society . . . for we have seen among several peoples who have been recently liberated, that the woman, once free, starts to think of things which one need not cite here . . . which in no way have to do with social progress; quite the contrary . . . the evolution of Algerian woman and enjoyment of her rights must be in the framework of the morality of our society.'

Said she, Zubayda: 'Ya umma, listen to me!'

Said she, Jamila: 'You know what happens to little girls as ill-mannered as you. O mother Rahma, bring us one the same!'

And Zubayda screamed, and Jamila ran from the room and took a red shawl and covered her head and returned, beating the door with a stick and crying that the ogre Bululu hath come!

Bululu!

Whereupon mother and daughter hugged each other and wept copious tears of alarm.

Bi-llahi! And time waxed straight and Jamila's heart straightened with it; and the last remains of the Emir Abd al-Qadir were ceremonially returned to Algiers from Damascus where he had died in exile, internationally respected eighty-five years afore. And presently Zubayda was to begin secondary school and her grandmother, panicky that PE might require some unnatural stretch or position, and so jeopardize hope for a marriage with honour, hurried her to the doctor to quietly procure a certificate of virginity, as an ultimate safeguard should this be. Meanwhile, Hadj Bashir was at the office pushing a pen and piles of paper, and somewhere his father wheeled and dealed dinars, which had proved excellent therapy for his heart. Jamila emptied a wardrobe. She went down the stairs to the kitchen and disconnected the gas cylinder from the cooker, and dragged it to her room, and levered it into the cupboard.

She climbed inside and sat and pulled shut the door. The air smelt of moth balls. The darkness gave her courage.

She turned on the gas. It hissed, O so soothingly. She remembered his beautiful eyes, and she fingered the deerskin talisman which hung about her neck, and soon her dear heartbeat slowed to a stop.

All is Allah's Decree . . . but from this sadness let me hastily flee.

Now, it has reached me that one day it chanced that Satan appeared before an Algerian sowing his fields.

Said he, the Devil: 'Half the world belongs to me. Thus I have a right to half of the crop planted by thee.'

Said he, the Algerian: 'But which half? The half below ground, or the half above?'

Now Satan, though skilled in a variety of ways, was no agronomist. Could he tell a pumpkin from a turnip seed? La! However, he was not about to be fobbed off with the roots, and so he chose the half above ground.

The harvest came and it was a plenteous season, and Satan appeared with his usual thunderclap and smoke and other sensationalisms, and the Algerian presented him with a pile of green turnip-tops, good if boiled, but otherwise fit for cattle. And when Satan saw these, he was wroth with exceeding wrath and his reason wellnigh fled as indeed has my memory about what next occurred.

'Sahha! A few more of our douros—'

'—no need, my friends, for I know the story well. Half the amount will loosen my tongue—'

—al-hamdu li-llah, unaided my mind seems quite refreshed, and said he, the Devil: 'O dog, shall the like of thee treat me thus? Who art thou? At the very next harvest I will return and woe be to thee if I cannot claim the half which has grown below ground.'

And Satan returned, and found that the Algerian had planted a crop of buckwheat, and he took flight, vowing to have nothing more to do with our nation.

Wah! Know O my brothers, that Life is no more than a turning and a returning without repose.

Now, as regards to Azallah Boudjemaa; he stood and waited for Yamina outside the railway station in Constantine. Torn clouds raced in a fierce blue sky. Chevrons of birds flew north. A man offered to shine his cowboy boots, but someone at that moment called his name.

Azallah turned. She was swathed in a black haik and wore a white veil. Without a further word they began to stroll, up towards the hospital and where the span of the Sidi M'Sid bridge strung gracefully from cliff edge to cliff edge across the gorge yonder to the old town and high Kasbah. And

Azallah and Yamina were tied to each other tight by some invisible thread as strong and as soft as silk.

Then on a bench they sat, and people passed, and a one-way stream of cars flowed across the ravine, and a winnowing breeze blew cool and sweet, and at last Yamina voiced this sorry soliloquy.

Said she, Yamina: 'When I was sixteen I was married and on my wedding night as the cries of *you-you* became ever stronger and my husband entered, I broke an egg on the floor to prevent being dominated by him for all my life. Now, my husband was handsome and of perfect symmetry and with face like the sun shining in the sheeny sky, and he was kind, and I was happy and cheerful and glad. He owned a small-holding and there we lived in peace and splendid isolation, and then six Ramadans ago it was collectivized as part of the Agrarian Revolution, and we were regrouped into one of the socialist villages along with other families in the vicinity, and like them we wept tears like rain and almost drowned in the sea of our solicitudes and said nay, but the military moved us, we had no choice, and as a result I miscarried our first child.

'There were a hundred houses in the village, a fifth would have been enough, all built of concrete and fired brick, each with two rooms and a small courtyard, and their outward-facing windows opened on to wide straight roads. There was a mosque, a school, a shop, a café, a post-office and a hammam, and at night street-lamps would cast an eerie glow. And when we were settled the village was opened officially by the President Boumédienne himself, and how I recall that day. The sky was massed with clouds. Flags hung everywhere, and there was a feast with food enough for a year, with trays of the richest viands of all kinds. And then there was a speech which said that the village enabled us to *enter the school of communal and co-operative life by which it would guarantee the construction of a true socialist society*, and I remember those words, odd, for I know not why.

'Now my husband was independent by nature, and did not take to production controlled by the state. He missed his small-holding, and how morose and lethargic he was to become. And the facilities in the village made him restless for they smelt of the city, and so one night when the rondure of the moon was at its full we left and walked to sunrise when we took the first bus, which brought us here to Constantine.

'Now my husband trudged the city for hours each day, but was unable to find employ. We built our home out of boxes, corrugated iron, and even a rusting car door, not far from here at Faubourg Lamy near the old Jewish cemetery. And there I gave birth to a child.

'Then somewhere he found work, but as time passed he gave me next to no money, but now and again brought home a sack of semolina and two kilos of chick peas and I was supposed to be happy with my lot.

'One day in front of witnesses my husband repudiated me, and left for I know not where, someone said Algiers, another said France. I had no male relatives to go to. My daughter . . . she died. I was alone.

'And I had no choice.'

And Azallah was mute and said naught. Yamina remained motionless, but felt inwardly the urge to do something drastic: to scream like the wind in the mountains on a savage winter night; to stab a knife into her chest as men stabbed themselves into her several times each day; to jump as the criminals of old were thrown, far down into the rush of the Rhummel.

Presently, they crossed the suspension bridge and walked along the Rue Marium Bouattoura, passing by the piquancy of restaurants sizzling liver and mutton brochettes over charcoal fires, to where the road dipped towards the Hôtel de Ville. Whereupon, they turned down a side-street and into the hum and bustle of a restaurant there, though its ceiling in part had collapsed and its pieces swept into the corner. The white-haired and -moustached proprietor showed them to a small alcove with a table and four chairs, and swished a curtain closed to conceal them.

Yamina threw back her haik and untied her lace-edged veil. She noticed the pin-prick scarring each ear-lobe of Azallah, and leant slightly over to massage one with her forefinger and thumb.

Said he, Azallah: 'Tiny gold spheres. For good luck.'

And he smiled his boyish heart-catching smile.

Thus far concerning them; but as regards Hadj Bashir Ben Nassif he beat his face and tore at his clothes for he had all but lost his wits; and he saw Jamila in each and every expression and deed of Zubayda as if forever in judgement, and he repeated over and over, 'God does not charge a soul with more than it can bear.' And he tried to web his daughter with paternal love, but she was wilful and also of the age when girls take an attitude of prudery vis-à-vis their fathers, and anyway it was just too late, and presently Hadj Bashir took an invitation to work in the Ministry of —— in Algiers, and left his child in the care of her grandmother and her aunts.

Whereupon a decade passed, in which Zubayda outmanoeuvred her grandmother and chose for marriage a man with nondescript looks but modern ideas, and her father rocketed to the very galaxy of government in a series of spectacular promotions, and painful memories faded. The decade passed, and thereupon the earth rumbled and razed the town of Al Asnam to the ground, and with a jolt Hadj Bashir knew it to be a sign.

Twenty-five years.

Twenty-five years before Al Asnam had been called Orléansville. And twenty-five years ago the earthquake at Orléansville had been the drum roll which had heralded the end of the long colonial night, and the dawn of our revolution.

Twenty-five years on and Algeria's indulged and quixotic childhood had ended, as the publication of the Charte Nationale touched off a taper to feelings of disillusionment and discontent with the upbringing by her various guardians.

Twenty-five years, and two thirds of the national population was under twenty-five years old. Yet how many had access to fast cars and Levi jeans and Nike trainers apart from the *chi chis*, the children of the incumbent and veteran revolutionaries?

Twenty-five years. And lo! violent riots broke out in Tizi-Ouzo as the Berbers demanded the recognition of their own language and their own culture too.

Now, Hadj Bashir saw that as the threshold to worse. How long before the tanks moaned and gunfire resounded once again in the streets of Algiers? Indeed, how long would it be before *scorpion fought scorpion*?

Wa-llahi! The earth rumbled and razed the town of Al Asnam to the ground, and this time it was renamed Ech Cheliff.

But Hadj Bashir knew this to be mere semantics, certain that it was just a matter of Time.

And so, and so on for days his mind raged like a tempest at sea, until he set off on a mission to Cairo, and after a touch-down at Tunis en route his red-bearded neighbour left the aeroplane clicking a rosary of amber beads, and behind him, forgotten on the seat, lay a translation of Farid ud-Din Attar's *The Conference of the Birds*. And they took off, and the hostess served lunch, and Hadj Bashir read these extempore verses:

The hoopoe said: 'How arrogant you are
To think your wretched self so singular!
The disappointments of this world will die
In less time than the blinking of an eye
And as the earth must pass, pass by the earth—
Don't even glance at it, know what it's worth;
What empty foolishness it is to care
For what must one day be dispersed to air . . .'

And outside the cabin window the sky was as fervid a red as fire, and the flight began a lengthy descent to Cairo, and Hadj Bashir read:

Another bird said: 'Hoopoe, you can find
The way from here, but we are almost blind—
The path seems full of terrors and despair.
Dear hoopoe, how much further till we're there?'

'Before we reach our goal,' the hoopoe said,
'The journey's seven valleys lie ahead;
How far this is the world has never learned,
For no one who has gone there has returned—
Impatient bird, who would retrace this trail?
There is no messenger to tell the tale,
And they are lost to our concerns below—
How can men tell you what they do not know?
The first stage is the Valley of the Quest;
Then love's wide valley is our second test;

The third is Insight into Mystery,
The fourth Detachment and Serenity—
The fifth is Unity; the sixth is Awe,
A deep bewilderment unknown before,
The seventh Poverty and Nothingness—
And there you are suspended, motionless.
Till you are drawn – the impulse is not yours—
A drop absorbed in seas that have no shores.

And hence Hadj Bashir completed his businesses of state in Egypt, and returned to Constantine and the Ben Nassif villa at Bellevue, but tears of joy were soon superseded by strangled cries of shock, woe and sorrow as he sketched his religious intentions, and then took himself upstairs where he stripped a room of all its trappings. Out the window went a mattress, curtains, lamp and chairs; out the door went a bed and chest of drawers. And all manner of fatal ailments were feigned by his family to forfend such dogged resolutions, but nevertheless Hadj Bashir remained in the room with his head bowed in meditation. Then there was a rap at the door, and it opened, and there stood Zubayda, with his youngest grandson at her side.

Said she, Zubayda: 'Ya baba! Come outside and see your grandchildren, for they are verily works of God!'

Said he, Hadj Bashir: 'Daughter: come inside to contemplate the Creator. Contemplation of the Creator prevents me from contemplating what has been created.'

Whereupon he remained, and cast himself upon God to let him abandon his social eminence and all his family. Then one sunrise, which had shot the sky with the rubescence of a blazing pyre, he clad himself in a white burnous, and set out to bear witness that there is no reality but the Reality, the Divine Oneness, and that all else is His shadow, and thus began a lifelong peregrination in which he sought annihilation in God.

And on to that I tag: amen!

You all look stunned, stunned as a man just stung by a bee! So I flit on, to Azallah. He strode, and the day was dying. His mind tumbled. From his breath winter phantoms condensed and vanished, yet the air was zested with the scent of spring.

Or was it love?

'No, it is impossible.'

'Why?'

'How can you love a woman deflowered, and more, a common prostitute.'

'He's right!'

'Bi-llah. The heart of the fool is in his mouth, and the mouth of the wise man is in his heart.'

'Ya Rahwun, ignore them and go on.'

'A few coins to help you go on: here!'

Love.

The thought disturbed him. His grandfather had many times told him to take heed of the vulgar proverb, 'even the straightest of women is twisted like a sickle'. Therein lay an element of prophecy.

First he had been the victim of a conspiracy cooked up by his married sister, Assia, and worse, his own mother!

Said she, Assia: 'Life was so sweet before the baby was born! Now my husband works so hard that I never see him.'

Said she, Nadia: 'Al-hamdu li–llah! With a child you need all the extra money your husband can find.'

Nadia held a sieve almost to her chin as she sorted lentils for she refused to have her eyes tested for glasses.

Said she, Assia: 'But my husband needs help in his restaurant—'

Said she, Nadia: '—I see your problem. You want people to eat your food, not your profits!'

Said she, Assia: 'Exactly. We could send for his mother from Tunisia. That would give me more free time.'

Said he, Azallah: 'Ya umma! It should be you who goes to help with the baby!'

Said she, Nadia: 'No . . . my place is with you my son, at least until you marry, inshallah! Who will make your meals and wash your clothes?'

Said he, Azallah: 'D'accord.'

And ho!: Nadia and Assia exchanged rapid glances.

Said she, Nadia: 'Yes, your father would have wished it so. And what interest does an old woman like me have in watching my grandson grow?'

Said he, Azallah: 'Ya umma! This is unnatural. My father would have wanted you to go, I am sure of it!'

Said she, Nadia: 'But Lyon is so far away from Paris . . .'

But Azallah had insisted, and his mother had finally been persuaded to move.

Whereupon, two months later, he had chanced to see Assia interviewed on the television news, as the new vice-president of a Maghrebi women's movement busy in the suburbs of Lyon.

Azallah coloured as he remembered, and walked on, passed the corrugated-metal and stone-secured tarpaulin-roofed wooden-walled shacks of a bidonville hugging a quarry edge, and passed a long slab of flats, and then down a muddy road edged by a higgledy-piggledy of houses self-built in grey breeze-blocks.

And as regards Azallah's other sister: she lived, unmarried, with a Frenchman.

Yet.

Yamina repelled him, yet attracted him. She was unvirtuous, yet good. She was so strong, and yet so weak. She was corrupted, but innocent. Her spirit was dark, eclipsing a soul ablaze. There was a sourness about her, matched by some quality so sweet. She ordered his passions, yet threw him in chaos. Fever engulfed him, yet she chilled his heart. In this way, she seemed to have gently stirred some dormant truth about himself.

Meanwhile, in another part of the city, Yamina's client lay silently asleep. She decided to give him a little more time. She crossed the room, and opened the cardboard folder he had laid on the dressing table. Inside was a photograph stapled to a blue card which gave access to the Archives of the Wilaya of Constantine, and she read his transliterated name: Michel Juan Ardales. American. There was a letter written in English on writing paper from the best hotel in Constantine, the *Cirta*, but begun, *Chérie*. There was an *Iberia* airticket Los Angeles–Madrid–Los Angeles, returning the following month. And then Yamina flicked through the exercise book beneath, and the squared feint of the pages seemed damasked by the sepia ink and the garlanded longhand, and they contained much flimflam some of which I now improvise in all its wacky manner!

1849. Préfecture built.

Asterisk. Extracts of letters from the General Saint-Arnaud, Commander of Constantine, to his son.

20th to 25th July 1850.

I have added to my menagerie two lions, Juba and Cirta . . . they are charming, playing like cats, following like dogs. Nothing is more comic than their game with the monkeys: these latter pass friendly inspections of their manes. When Juba, weary of these liberties he suffers, menaces and snarls, the monkeys, in two bounds, reach the top of the column and, from there, insult the king of animals. The gazelles, the ostrich, the swans dread the moment when my lions parade in the garden, and, when they do, the dogs refuse to go there . . .

Cholera surrounds us, but does not worry us.

12th to 22nd February 1851.

The balls continue at Constantine. There are three this week, it's a little too much.

7th to 12th March 1851.

We have closed the soirées and Carnival honourably by a beautiful ball, gay, animated, and which has met unanimous approval, rare thing here as everywhere. Illuminations à giorno, tapestries, hangings, coloured glasses, flowers and greenery coiled round columns and under arcades of galleries [at the Palace of Bey Hadj Ahmed]. Flakes of snow fell, covering the ground and the orange trees of the garden, making a magnificent contrast. Nothing was missing, it was fairylike, one drank, ate, danced until six in the morning, and one finished the day with a snowball fight. The grace and dress of Louise [his wife] was delightful: she was a credit to her palace and her ball.

1854. Municipality built.
Architect? Try Mercier, *Histoire de Constantine* (1903) or: Valler, *Constantine, son passé, son centenaire 1837–1937*

GET PHOTOCOPY.

Grande Mosque partially destroyed and rebuilt 1865 for new alignment of the Rue Nationale.

1883. Theater.

1894. Mayor of Constantine, Cassanove. Exclamation mark. Municipality installs a brothel next to the Grande Mosque. Petition to Governor General on 8th July, complaining that Friday sermons were disturbed by songs, laughter and obscenities in a loud voice . . . CHECK ARCHIVES NATIONALES D'ALGÉRIE.

Croix-de-Feu Movement in city. Right-wing oblique fascist. The Ku Klux Klan of French Algeria question mark.
Check.
N.B. Same time *l'affaire Dreyfus* being played out in Paris.
Arrow: Napoleon III gave orders for the levelling and development of Koudiat Aty facing old city.
Commenced 1896.
Completed 1930.

Question mark. Wasn't ISABELLE EBERHARDT in Constantine circa 1900 during the trial of her assailant Abdallah Muhammad. Question mark.

Casino built blank. Find date. Now Maison de la Culture.

1934. Constantine scene of pogrom between 2nd and 6th August.
23 Jews, 3 Muslims killed.
81 injured.
Blamed by left-wing press on French colonial admin., military activity, fascist propaganda and imperialist influence in city.

SOCIAL ECOLOGY question mark.

Scribble scored out.

STATS. 1837. Built up area Const. 30 hectares equals question mark acres.
1937. 239 hectares.
Ditto. Europeans less than 50 per cent of urban pop but occupy 80 per cent of municipal land. Military 25 per cent of 80. Seems city difficult to control.

GROSS DENSITIES: Muslims: 1,428 persons per hectare.
Europeans: 279 p.p.h.

1954 100,000 Muslims in shanty towns on periphery of city.

85 per cent European pop with water in dwelling.
18 per cent Muslim pop ditto.

Frantz Fanon. 1961. *The Wretched of the Earth*. General, dash.

The settler's town is a strongly-built town, all made of stone and steel. It is a brightly-lit town; the streets are covered with asphalt, and the garbage-cans swallow all the leavings, unseen, unknown, and hardly thought about . . . The settler's town is a well-fed town, an easy-going town; its belly is always full of good things. The settler's town is a town of white people, of foreigners. The town belonging to the colonised people . . . is a place of ill fame, peopled by men of evil repute. They are born there, it matters little where or how; they die there, it matters not where, nor how. It is a world without spaciousness; men live there on top of each other . . . The native town is a hungry town, starved of bread, of meat, of shoes, of coal, of light. The native town is a crouching village, a town on its knees, a town wallowing in the mire. It is a town of niggers and dirty Arabs.

Fanon. '59 *Towards the African revolution.* On Constantine,

The colonisers have surrounded the native city; they have laid seige to it. Every exit . . . opens onto enemy territory.

Thereupon, Yamina closed the exercise book, for the pages were mere impressions which meant nothing to her, and she replaced it carefully in the folder, and she bent by the bed to shake her client awake.

'Ya Rahwun! Have you another fable to tell?'

Bi-llahi. I am in a gloomy, but obliging mood.

They recount that in the capital, in the Kasbah, is the house of She-Who-is-Made-Up. And there there lived two sisters, and the first was sensible and traditional, and she had married a good businessman, and became a good mother. However, the second was youthful and beautiful and charming, and she sang and she danced and she played the tambourine, and she made up her eyes with charcoal dust, and rubbed her cheeks with rose-hued rice powder to set off her lily complexion. And all the men in the kasbah watched for her, and this seemed so scandalous that her brother-in-law ordered his wife to break relations with her sister.

Now, the younger sister was the co-owner of the house, and lived in a room in the basement, having rented out the others, and when her brother-in-law had a fit and demanded that she leave, for her sister's sake she sadly agreed. Whereupon the elder sister prepared a fabulous final supper, and soon the aroma of tripe and vegetables filled the house and therein the lodging rooms.

And amongst these rooms lived a pregnant girl, whose husband was very poor, and she passed back and forth before the door of the kitchen with eyes that danced with envy.

Said she, the younger sister: 'Sister, share our meal with this poor wretch.'

Said she, the elder sister: 'We cannot feed lodgers.'

Said she, the younger sister: 'By Allah! I'll give you my half of the house in payment if you feed this woman. This is my last night here!'

Well, the pact was concluded, and the poor lodger was fed, and then they themselves fell to eating and drinking and attempts at making merry. And then the two sisters parted for the night, and the youngest descended to her chamber on the lower most floor.

Then the next day dawned, and the elder sister found the door to this room closed, and water flowing mysteriously from beneath it. And she opened it, and entered.

'Wa-llahi! Time to empty our purses!'

I merely paused for a cigarette, my friend! But Allah will reward you for your benevolence . . .

'Here's a coin.'

'And another two.'

Sahha! Does anybody have a cigarette? Shukran!

Hhmmm. Hem. Hh hh hehh.

And lo! there she discovered her sister wound carefully with white winding sheets and ritually washed by supernatural hands, her young features set in a brilliant beauty. And the air of the bedchamber was heavy with a heavenly perfume, and the elder sister fell to the floor and humbled herself before God and wept lavish tears, and thereupon demanded that her sister be buried in that very room so that she never left the house with whose gift she had made payment for Eternity. And know, O my brothers, that a sojourn in the room brings good luck, and a crude knock at its door makes a melodious sound. Moreover, on certain days, witnesses have testified that the air is scented with a celestial perfume.

Now, after a little trouble, Azallah Boudjemaa found the Office National Algérien de Main d'Oeuvre, ONAMO. He was directed to the Service de Réinsertion and there introduced to a comely youth who imparted with a rattle the following information.

Said he: 'Shall we continue to speak in French? It's

probably easier for you. Now if you are returning to Algeria, inshallah!, you can import a car plus your family belongings free of customs duty. If you're a doctor or a dentist you may bring in equipment tax-free too. You're a baker? No, sorry, that isn't classified as a liberal profession. I think. I'll check. But ONAMO can provide a loan to help you set up in business. Or perhaps you would prefer to be enrolled in a six-month training programme? Agricultural mechanics, mechanical engineering and metallurgy, secretarial work, take your pick. The drawback is that if you do, you forfeit the repatriation allowance. What I can do is allocate you a flat as ONAMO is given a quota of all new housing projects. I've no one else to see today, so if you like I'll take you and show you one.'

Whereupon they left the building and drove across the city, and the youth still chattered on merrily.

Said he: 'Buy a BMW if you can. For the prestige. Failing that you could settle for a Peugeot 504 or a Renault 5 but, if the latter, get the version with five doors. Avoid at all costs the Fiat Supermiafiori or a Honda, as they mark you as Moudjahid or military, respectively. Four years ago I applied for a car to SONACOM, and am still waiting. So last month I gave up, and bought this Renault 16 in the secondhand car market held on the Brèche on Fridays. The price was 90,000 dinars. Naʿam! More than the cost of a new one, but that's life! What was that? Why are such things here so difficult? The old hate the young. That's what I think.

'Now housing is a problem in Constantine. I have a few sticky facts at my finger tips. The Second Four Year Plan, that is '74 to '77, allocated six thousand dwelling units to be built in Constantine, but yet less than half had been completed by last year, 1980! If you teach in higher education you are guaranteed being allocated a flat . . . there's something wrong with these gears . . . where was I? Ah. Nearly all primary and secondary school teachers are also allocated flats. The odds are more like 50:50 if you work for some state enterprise or another. But if you can use “le piston”, string-pulling, that is another matter. Failing that you’re left to resourcefulness, that’s right, “Système D”. Five or six years ago the law gave the commune the monopoly in buying and selling land for development. Some was zoned for private use, and my family decided to pool their resources and buy a plot. We had enough money for the land, but were then told that we would have to build our house within three years from the date of purchase. Well, we’re not millionaires! If they could have deferred building for five years, well . . . here we are.

‘Across this earth, it’ll be landscaped soon, inshallah! Up these stairs . . . now which key? Right first time! Bathroom to the right, and then through to the living room. You can easily cover up those big windows. This door here goes off to the kitchen, and that door to a bedroom, quite large isn’t it? And this door goes into an adjoining room which leads back into the living room so! Of course, furniture in Algeria is expensive, and as for the price of electrical equipment . . . Bring all you can, and buy more than one of everything, as you can then sell the spare items here for five times what you paid. In fact, if I gave you some money, I’ve got francs, perhaps you would buy me one or two things in France and bring them across for me as well?’

And they returned to the city centre, and Azallah thanked him, and farewelling him, fared on.

Whereupon I too shall take my leave, but before I do I give you this to guess:

> A bird takes flight with a fast horseman;
> Its plumage is black and its heart is iron.

Shukran . . . shukran!

Glory be to the Living who dieth not and in whose hand are the Keys of the Seen and Unseen!

The Tenth

My young cousin is studying at the University of Constantine. Is he to be a doctor, an engineer, an economist or a lawyer? My uncle wept until he was senseless on learning that, calamity of calamities, his son was set to study geography. I did remind him that Muslims have always been great travellers and very early on introduced method to the study of geography: for instance, scientific cartography was developed in the Islamic world. What of such names as al-Masudi, al-Idrisi and al-Yaqubi? What of Ibn Battuta and his chronicle of travel from Tangiers to far-off Asia? But such arguments were all to no avail.

But I digress. My cousin told me this: his department is situated in the old military hospital, in the kasbah. Now, one of his colleagues arrived one morning driving a present from his father . . . a car! The aged attendant, a former Moudjahid, refused to raise the barrier across the gate as he had no parking permit. The boy leapt out. An argument followed. The attendant was resolute. In a fury, the boy snatched up a rock and struck the old man on the head.

He died, allah irahmu, before idh-dhur prayer.

'Ya Rahwun. The answer to the riddle.'
'Has it blood or not?'
It can draw blood: it is a rifle that is the word of the riddle.

In the name of Allah, the Compassionate, the Merciful!

Azallah Boudjemaa watched the patterns of light across the hotel room. The panes of the windows were casting mottled ragged patterns on the walls. Parallelograms slipped into trapezoids. Trapezoids slipped back into parallelograms. Distortions in the glass rippled the wall with cataracts and Azallah slipped into drowsiness and his body felt as insubstantial as the light. Then the tonalities of grey around him were inflamed by a range of colour, a palette reminiscent of Paris, with its universe of illuminants, its hoardings and advertisements, its clothes and fashions, its shops, and . . . its flans and tarts, topped by overlapped or spiralled apple slices, or patterned by circles of sliced bananas, halved grapes and plums glossed with apricot glaze. Beyond the rose-veined marble counter of the local pâtisserie, Azallah would in his early youth glimpse the men wrapped and capped in white, rolling dough, cutting it into triangles, then lifting each up and spinning it between two hands into a croissant. Wa-llah!

How many of us in the carefree days of childhood were fascinated to see our mothers seated on the floor before the mound of semolina in a large wooden or metal flat dish, and after pushing her slim gold bangles up her forearm, watch as her left hand would add cold salted water from a ladle whilst the fingers of the right travelled in sweeping circles, only pausing to spill in a handful of flour and so on, and so forth, until the ingredients were mixed and globular, and thereupon shaken through a round flat sieve to shower thousands of grains of couscous ready to be dried, then stored . . . Ahh, ya hasra.

'Ya Rahwun, my family uses a different method. Instead of—'

'—making it, you buy it in packets!'

And if you've all laughed loudly long enough—

'Ya Rahwun, talking of food, I give you this to guess:

Red as blood,
It stings like poison.

'Shall I give you a clue?'

Another one? No need, for I ken that the answer is a red pepper. And now that your smiles have gone, I shall go on.

Now Azallah ever felt a quickening of the pulse by the aromas of vanilla, lemon, sugar, and baking in the pâtisserie, and by persistence found someone to take him as an apprentice to learn this art, an exact art. Note: 1.3 kilograms of dough are required to make twenty croissants. Pâte feuilletée fine has equal quantities of butter and flour, six rollings out and six foldings, to give seven hundred and twenty-nine layers of butter a-sandwiched between seven hundred and thirty layers of dough. All this, and the skills and secrets of bavaroises, soufflés, bombes, charlottes, mousses, marzipan fruits, cats, owls, and roses, spun sugar, and petits-fours and more Azallah had learnt to receive his *Certificat d'Apprentissage Professionnel de Pâtissier*. And he was content and sure in the knowledge that for each item he made he brought a moment of pleasure and happiness to young and old alike. He could not give this up, which I am sure you all will fathom.

And Azallah was so beset by confusion, for it had crossed his mind to marry Yamina. Yet to stay in Constantine would be a problem, unless she remained veiled outside the home, as someone might recognize her, and that could perhaps affect business. But where could he open a pâtisserie? There were no shops near the blocks of flats he had been shown. Maybe he could try Algiers, where his family were sure to welcome him, and string-pull like mad. But would they welcome Yamina? And one other thought niggled him: was Yamina capable of bearing him children?

Azallah left the hotel. The afternoon air was fresh and thin beneath a mackerel sky. His road led him past the rear entrance to the Nouvelles Galleries Algériennes, where two queues, one single line of men, one of women, fanned out into the street.

He a-rendezvoused with Yamina by the post-office, and they strolled together down to the Avenue Aouti Mustafa towards the Hôtel Panoramique, and turned into a salon de thé. The ceiling was low, and the room centred by a large rectangular counter spread with sponge cakes, small almond moons, date lozenges and mille feuilles, all overlooked by a gallery and to this, up the stairs, they went. Music from the English singers, the Beatles, was being played, and at the various small square tables young lovers sat. Yamina lifted off her haik, but kept on her veil. They ordered mint tea, and it was brought in an ornate silver pot. Azallah began to talk of Paris, and he became suddenly annoyed at not seeing more than the eyes of Yamina's face.

Said he, Azallah: 'Why don't you come and see for yourself. We'll leave tomorrow or the day after. Whenever there is a flight. We'll get married. It'll be a fresh start.'

Yamina placed her red-lacquered finger tips over his nails, all bitten to the quick.

Said she, Yamina: 'In Paris you will see me with different eyes—'

Said he, Azallah: '—I'll be able to see you.'

Said she, Yamina: 'I must leave you now.'

She rose and made to go. But Azallah grasped her wrist, tighter than he meant, and asked her once again to come to Paris and be his wife.

Finally Yamina agreed, but did so with a secret laid heavy in her heart.

Then Azallah was overcome with a cold flush of betrayal, for he recalled that his grandfather Hadj Ali had years before instructed him on the Promise and the Pledge.

Said he, Hadj Ali: 'Ya Azallah, remember this: a man without honour is no man. Therefore it is wise to have a neck as long as a camel, so that when words leave your heart, they have a long way to travel to the tongue, giving you time to reflect. For words are like bullets shot from a rifle: they cannot come back.'

Now they paid and left and walked at a reflective pace, a deathly hush between them in the approaching twilight, and the two arrived at Air Algérie, and entered in and three men and one young woman were behind the computer terminals there installed. Their turn soon came, and they sat themselves before the girl whose hair was as black as a well in which a thousand lovers fell, whose face had a radiant grace which outshone the moon, whose eyebrows' curve was like a bow arched and drawn in doom, above dark and humid eyes and cheeks of rosen light, and teeth like marguerite and lips like ruby. And on her desk the nameplate read: Zubayda Ben Nassif.

Said he, Azallah: 'We'd like two one-way tickets to Paris on the first available flight.'

Zubayda rattled the keyboard with delicate hands.

Said she, Zubayda: 'There're places available on one in ten minutes. Can I confirm?'

And she laughed a laugh of nectar.

Said he, Azallah: 'Tomorrow.'

Said she, Zubayda: 'Tomorrow morning. Could I have your names please, passport numbers and in your case, Monsieur, proof of having completed your military service if you are resident in Algeria?'

There was a pause. Yamina leant across to Azallah, and whispered what he had suspected: she had no passport.

Whereupon they arose without a word, Azallah hot with rage. It was Yamina who turned with the courtesy to say 'Sahha!'

And Zubayda smiled part-puzzled as she watched them leave, and touched the deerskin talisman which hung around her neck, stark above the whiteness of her blouse.

And lo! Yamina pleaded with Azallah to forget all about her and hasten back to France. But Azallah said nay, for though she angered him she filled him with compassion, and he wished he could sweep her into his arms and hold her there, secure, for ever and a day. So he remained adamant that they would leave Constantine quickly and together to wherever, on the first available train.

Azallah pressed on, heading down to the Sidi Rashid bridge, and just behind Yamina followed, caught for breath. Falling tired beside them the jagged pantile roofs of the old city crumbled to derelict walls and foundations towards the cliff, ancient courtyards marked by single palms. Then further on the gorge screamed alongside them, howling in the dusk.

They crossed the Avenue Ali Zaamouche to the station, and there an enquiry through a ticket window revealed that there were trains at 22.20 (Rapide) and 23.50, to the capital. Yamina decreed these times impossible, and suggested that they leave Constantine at dawn by bus, and gave a time and a venue to meet, and then was gone, hurrying back in the nightfall towards the abyss.

Know, O my brothers, that that night Yamina slept a disturbed and fitful sleep in the cold darkness of her room, her heart rent by love, but her mind torn by ghoulish memories.

Now, her marriage had been recognized by their family and friends, and that had been deemed enough, and what need for paper proofs? And in this state she had borne her daughter Hajila, but when her husband repudiated her, as you all knoweth, the child was no longer a child but a bastard in the cataract vision of officialdom. Remarry, naʿam! But the second husband cannot recognize the girl. And more and moreover, Yamina was unable to enrol Hajila in school, for without documents ho! she could not obtain the requisite fiche familiaire.

With the last of her money she bought little Hajila a dress, red with white polka dots and puffed sleeves all trimmed with frills and fancies and lace, and for her dainty feet socks and plastic sandals. And Yamina brushed and wound her hair in twisted tresses gleaming black, and tied with ribbons like alighting butterflies. Thereupon they spent the day playing together, and walking round the city hand-in-hand and up to the nearby wooded slopes with the trees towering and the birds carolling, and Yamina entertained her with merry quips, and mirth-provoking sayings, and rare tales of which this is a fine example:

Kan ma kan.

One day that rascal Ben Sikran was in the market and he passed by a man selling dried figs. He tried one, and it was so sweet and good that he asked for a basket full. Then the vendor told him the price.

Said he, Ben Sikran: ‘Do me a kindness so that God may

show you a kindness too. Allow me to pay on the next market day.'

The vendor agreed.

Whereupon, the following week, Ben Sikran rubbed nettles over his face and hands until his skin was red and raw and swollen, and then he hobbled into the market with the aid of a staff. Reaching the vendor he stopped and spoke in a laboured and wheezing style.

Said he, Ben Sikran: 'Have you seen the whelp who sold me a basket of figs? Everyone in my village who tasted one died but me, and I'm going to whip him whilst I still can.'

Said he, the fig vendor: 'No, I haven't seen him.'

And so on till the evening came, and they returned to their shack, and Yamina set all manner of delicious delights and syrupy pastries before Hajila in the candlelight, and while she ate them Yamina mixed sleeping tablets into a beaker of hot milk, momentarily panicking for they refused to dissolve. And she gave it to Hajila to drink, and sat with her, singing softly, until she breathed no longer and her hand went cold.

Thus far as regards Yamina; and as regards Azallah, he had drowned in a dreamless sleep until awakened by the electronic bleep from his alarm, and for a moment he was near to rising to another life, for in the earliness of the hour was the spectre of France. His body ached with a slight stiffness as he climbed from the bed. He switched on the light. The inside of the window was patterned with frost-flowers. He washed and shaved and cleaned his teeth. He zipped shut his bag, and left the room, but half-turned back for a final glance.

A young boy unlocked the entrance to let him leave the hotel, and the henna door shut with a crash behind him and lo! in the deep of the starless night Constantine had been iced by falls of snow and was all powdered through with quiet, and the air was so brittle-sweet it seemed the air of aether, and awestricken for an instant Azallah stood, for it was a city of vanished dreams.

Beneath his feet the whiteness crunched and squeaked as he started the walk up Rue Larbi Ben M'Hidi, and he reached the café, but it was not yet open, but bathed in a yellow light with its chairs still stacked on its tables. He crossed the Place du 1 Novembre in a diagonal to the taxi rank, and waited.

'Ya Rahwun, you cannot fail us there!'

'Will Yamina tell him?'

'The glint of a few douros should dazzle him from his trance, inshallah! Here.'

'And this.'

'This too.'

'Have you change for a ten-dinar note?'

Sahha! Someone came hurrying across the square in the

silver light of the dawn. Azallah tensed and took a step forwards; but it was not she. He relaxed, and wondered if Yamina had gone directly to the bus station. He told the first of the waiting taxis to take him there, and off they slowly drove, and Azallah carefully brushed the snow off the edges of his boots.

Said he, the taxi driver: 'Wa-llah! You'll be lucky if you leave the city today: last year when it snowed, Constantine was cut off for three days! The airport is closed, that I know. Are you catching any bus in particular because I can't drive much faster. Wah! I see you're in luck: that bus just passing us is going off to Skikda.'

Thereupon they arrived at the bus station, and Azallah paid and walked the length of the concourse but there was no sign of Yamina. He bought two tickets, flimsy and white and initialled SNTV, for the next bus to depart, south to El Oued.

'El Oued!'
Aywa!

The bus left Constantine under a lead-grey sky. The acne-faced youth who sat beside Azallah was nervous, continually unfolding and reading his call-up paper for military service in Ouargla. Azallah gazed unseeing through the window. In his hand, between finger and thumb, was the ticket he had bought for Yamina, held like a petal of white cyclamen in danger of being bruised. Yet Azallah was not bedarkened by melancholy but lucent with joy, for her action had allowed him a measure of dignity. Moreover, he realized that Yamina had brought together the contraposition of culture and of language which had rendered so uncertain each gesture of his life, and somehow fused herself with this as if they were soda and sand, producing a glass which burst open the windowless wall of the nations which had imprisoned him, and let him see that he had only to be true to himself.

Ahead a shroud of ashen cloud streamed rain upon veiled mountains, and a glittering beam of sunlight gilded pinnacles of rock as the bus approached the Gorge of Al-Kantara. Through the rift, full in front, the Sahara flushed in the zenith of noon. Gone were the grey-green shrubs and the sombre mountain rock, replaced by stately groves of palms and an endlessness of honey sand. Briefly the bus stopped at Biskra, and then continued, the sand rising and falling in dunes as they neared El Oued, and it was the first time Azallah had seen the desert, and the emptiness thereabouts lent him refuge.

The bus drove into the city of a thousand white domes beneath a water blue sky, and Azallah took his bag and walked round towards Le Souf Hôtel which they had passed en route in. There he registered, and a porter took him past a courtyard with a swimming pool, and to a room on the first floor with a private bathroom on the left as he entered. He changed into a swimming costume which he had brought, and went down with a towel towards the pool where the air was heavy with chlorine and oil. Several French tourists lounged in chairs. He lay down and stretched out and soon the heat of the afternoon seemed to consume his body, pressing him like a weight. Behind his closed eyelids ran a restless redness with the transparency of flame, and around him each sound which broke the silence, whether a burst of water, a voice, a clink of ice in a glass, each seemed a crackle or fizzle from the fire which swallowed him until slowly he disintegrated into a heavy torpor, his mind free from thought.

Presently he sat up, and squinted his eyes at the shimmering turquoise of the pool. Two middle-aged couples had installed themselves on yellow loungers near by him, and the women bulged from bikinis and discussed their quest for souvenirs, and one of the men listened with rapt attention to the monologue of the other.

Said he, so-and-so: '. . . and it goes without saying that Napoleon III rewarded Saint-Arnaud, as his part in the coup d'état of 1851 was quite decisive. He was created a senator and a marshal of France. Then in 1854 he resigned his ministerial post, and though seriously ill, accepted the command of the French forces in the Crimea, and with the aid of Britain won the Battle of Alma, but then, sadly, he died nine or ten days after. His dying words were for the Emperor, and for his wife Louise. Strange enough, and I may be wrong, but I don't think there's any street in Paris named in his honour. After Bugeaud, yes. But Saint-Arnaud? No.'

And Azallah left, and showered, and that night in the restaurant ate heartily, and at the end of the meal realized that many days had passed without pains seizing his stomach. Thereupon he slept well, and in the early morning walked from the hotel and scrambled up to the crests of nearby dunes leaving a dimpled path from his hands and feet. On the top he sat and listened to the stillness, surrounded by sand, soft light, and deep shadow, and for some time there he stayed before returning down to the road.

A strong breeze blew sand about his ankles like serpents, and thus he walked along the asphalt until he reached the city. There he wound into the main square where men wandered about wrapped with white burnouses, examining sheep and haggling over one good or another. Then he passed a group, some sitting, some standing, some a-craning their necks towards the character they were gathered around, who sat cross-legged on the ground, before a circle drawn in the sand. Azallah looked mystified, and asked one of them who the man was.

Said he, the man: 'Rahwun. The story-teller.'

And I look at all of you around me and laugh. Now you too begin to smile and chuckle, and some even clap your hands with delight. And, al-hamdu li-llah! You shower more coins into the circle before me! I gather them up – nearly fifty dinars! – and I erase the circle with the palm of my hand so.

Say I, Rahwun: 'Sahha! The story is ended, spreading itself like a fire, a fire. And we, we have walked the length of the road, the road. Three apples leave Paradise: one is for me, the other for whosoever repeats this story, and as for the last, we shall split it, a little piece for each. Here is that we have understood and that we have said. And thee who burns for the very love of the Prophet, pronounce on him the salutation!'

'Blessings and greetings!'

Dossier: 3429/987–77
MUHAMMAD MADANI

Muhammad Madani: Thirty-two years. Born Debila. Son of Mafud Rashid and Benatia Fatma. Married with three children. Resident at Rue Hadj Umar, El Oued. Profession: lecturer at the University of Constantine until the riots of November 1986. Subsequently employed at El Souf. Arrested Sepember 1987. Condemned to death October 1987. Sentence commuted to life imprisonment July 1988. Held at Ouargla Prison, inmate number 3429. Principal charge: infraction of Article 77 of the Penal Code.

Hearing of Muhammad Madani by the Judge Farhat Bouzid, 13 October 1987 at 8.45 at Ouargla Prison (extract)

Question: Have you read the documents associated with your charge, which include the transcripts of your speeches in El Oued between the months of January and March of this year?

Response: I protest against the circumstances of my arrest. I have not received legal representation. The charges brought against me were made without a lawyer being present.

Question: You agree that you incited the citizens of El Oued to take up arms against the authority of the state?

Response: My aim was to further the cultural development and to record the history of our infant nation. The aim was not political. The Algerian constitution stipulates in Article 39: 'The fundamental liberties, and the Rights of Man and of the citizens, are guaranteed.'

Question: And what have you to say about the typewriter with French characters found in your home?

Response: It is for personal use only.

JUDGEMENT

Muhammad Madani.

Over a period of ten weeks he gave speeches with the aim to incite citizens to rise up in arms against the authority of the state or against fellow nationals. These speeches masqueraded as traditional stories, history, poetry, etc.

Concerning the typewriter in his possession, he denied that it had been used in the production of tracts and texts for public distribution, claiming that he had bought it for personal use.

He had been suspected by the security services of being behind the riots at Constantine in November 1986.

Verdict: Guilty.

October 1988

A burnt-out shell of a bus sat on its metal hubs on the street. A cash register lay on the pavement across a patch of dried blood. Slivers and fragments of glass had shattered everywhere from the government-run shops and agencies destroyed and looted by the rioters two days before. Ahead a soldier sat with a machine-gun on the turret of an olive and brown camouflaged tank, between white buildings, beneath a blue sky. Haddad turned into a building, painted with the slogan, YOUTH STAND UP! In the distance a gunshot cracked, and a police siren screamed.

Soldiers directed a group of civilians along a corridor, and into a room.

'Sir, a state of emergency has been declared, and there's to be a curfew from tonight, here in Algiers.'

'Thank you, Corporal. What are the latest figures?'

'Unofficial or official?'

'Unofficial.'

'Five hundred civilians dead. One thousand-plus injured. Nearly three thousand five hundred arrested.'

'Bring in the first of the accused.'

The corporal returned with a young man wearing blue trousers and a grey and white checked shirt, stained under the arms.

'Hassan Ben Ali, sir. Born Algiers, 1962. Son of Ali and Assouni Aicha. Single. Unemployed. Resident at Cité Fougeroux, Block 2, Bouzareah, Algiers. No previous record.'

'I refuse to recognize this military court!'

'Hassan Ben Ali: you are charged under Article 97 of the Penal Code with unarmed rioting in a public thoroughfare on Wednesday October 5.'

'We're tired of food shortages! We're tired of water rationing! We're tired of being unemployed! We're tired of corruption! We're tired . . .'

'This court finds you guilty, and sentences you to one year's imprisonment and a fine of two thousand five hundred dinars.'

'I refuse to recognize . . .'

The corporal steered the youth out. Haddad stood at the window. Across the street, on a wrought-iron balcony, a woman held a baby in her arms. Sixteen months he had been married, and still there was no sign of a child: he felt a rush of fury, picked up a chair, hurling it the length of the room where it clattered against the wall.

'Sir?'

'It's a bloody failure, Corporal. I thought that the arrests I helped the security services make last year, Muhammad Madani for one, would have stopped any uprising against the FLN. But the street-fighting has flared up in Blida, Tlemcen, Oran, Annaba, Ouargla, and who knows where else.' The corporal had returned the chair; his superior sank into it back behind the desk, and said petulantly: 'This job can be very dispiriting at times.'

'Yes, Captain Haddad. Shall I bring in the next prisoner, sir?'